UNNATURAL ORDER

edited by
Lyss Wickramasinghe
and
Alis Franklin

CS*f*G

Unnatural Order

Copyright 2020 by the Canberra Speculative Fiction Guild and the respective authors. All rights reserved, including the right to reproduce this book, or any portions thereof, in any form.

This is a work of fiction. All characters and events portrayed in this anthology are either fictitious or are used fictitiously.

Edited by Lyss Wickramasinghe and Alis Franklin.
Cover art by Jax Sheridan.

ISBN: 978-0-6484146-2-9 [hardcover]
       978-0-6484146-3-6 [paperback]
       978-0-6484146-4-3 [ebook]

National Library of Australia Cataloguing-in-Publication entry
Title: Unnatural Order / editor, Lyss Wickramasinghe and Alis Franklin.

CSFG Publishing
PO Box 1150
Dickson ACT 2602
Australia.

*To every monster,
and those that love them.*

More from the CSFG

A Hand of Knaves (2018)

The Never Never Land (2015)

Next (2013)

Winds of Change (2011)

Masques (2009)

The Outcast (2006)

Gastronomicon (2005)

Encounters (2004)

Elsewhere (2003)

Machinations (2002)

Nor of Human (2001)

Contents

Introduction and Acknowledgements ix

Full Steam Ahead 1
    Alexander Hardison

Truth Be Told 17
    Louise Pieper

Transcendence Inc. 29
    C.H. Pearce

Trench 49
    Nathan J Phillips

Emergent. 65
    DL Fleming

Mother of the Trenches. 77
    Grace Chan

The Scent of Olives 89
    Rob Porteous

Bruises Black and Blue 97
    Leife Shallcross

New Things 117
    Joanne Anderton

The Bargain 131
    Alannah K. Pearson

Eat Prey, Love 145
    Freya Marske

Crash Baby 161
    Donna Maree Hanson

The Lovers. 183
    Matthew Farrer

Meet Me at the Medusa 197
    Tansy Rayner Roberts

About the Authors 203

Introduction and Acknowledgements

We make our own monsters, then fear them
for what they show us about ourselves.
—M R Carey

Be it the dragon with its hoard, the shadow across the moon, or the kraken beneath the waves, monsters have always been an intrinsic part of speculative fiction. But rarely are they the focus. Which is a real shame; non-human characters are often some of the most engaging parts of a story, and are where we as writers get to flex our creative muscles. But often, the unique and the extraordinary are secondary because somehow they are viewed as less human. Not this time.

This time, it's the monsters' turn.

When Alis approached me with the idea to pitch an anthology to the Canberra Speculative Fiction Guild focusing on all the wild and weird creatures that feature in spec-fic, I jumped at the opportunity. The chance to explore the teeth and claws of spec-fic's plethora of monsters is always a good time, but it also gave us a chance to explore the ideas of human nature through the lens of something explicitly non-human. I have often empathised with the monsters in the stories I read, seeing pieces of myself behind the scales and spikes. This was the theme we wanted to explore: to observe humanity from the outside, the humanity of the inhuman. And our writers delivered more than we could have hoped.

Stories that explore the human mind, human heart and human soul; all without a human protagonist. Stories of friendship, new and old. Stories about longing and hope and frustration, about seeing the world from a different point-of-view. All told with a focus on creatures and beasts who are explicitly other, and what these things mean to them. We didn't want this anthology to become a collection of horror stories, so part of the selection process was finding a wide variety of pieces that explored the ideas of humanity and the monstrous from many different angles. It turned out to be far easier than we expected; apparently many people out there share our love of monsters.

The creation of this anthology hit a bump when 2020 decided to rear its nasty head and shut the whole world down. Worldcon was cancelled, CSFG meetings were moved online, and everyone had to focus inward as lock-downs and quarantines changed the game. But through all of this, we have muscled through and have brought this beast to life. And we couldn't have done it alone.

I, personally, would like to thank my truly spectacular co-editor, Alis Franklin. She is the real powerhouse behind this anthology, and none of it would exist without her. Thanks for bringing me along!

Together, we would like to thank Rivqa Rafael, our amazing publicity manager. Her experience and insight have been invaluable. And a huge thank you for showing us how Kickstarter works. That site is the true hell-beast.

Speaking of Kickstarter, we would like to thank all of our backers, for putting your money where your maw is, and having faith that this project was worth it. Special mention should go to Alis's mum for creating the adorable tentaplushies and proving to the world how cute tentacles can be.

Special thanks must also go to Elizabeth Fitzgerald; for proofing our manuscript in a very tight timeframe, and for putting up with us talking about creature-shaped shenanigans.

Thank you to our contributing writers, and everyone who submitted or shared your work with us, for taking our suggestions on board, and for reading the submission guidelines.

And thank you to the Canberra Speculative Fiction Guild. For looking at our pitch for this anthology and seeing the potential behind it. For the support and encouragement of your members, and for helping to fund this monster of a project.

And now you have well and truly stopped reading this, or are wondering when we get to the paws, maws and claws. So, I will say my final thank you to you, the reader, for purchasing this anthology. And I hope from the bottom of my monster-loving heart, that you enjoy it.

So, sink your teeth into Unnatural Order. It won't bite back… hard.

Lyss Wickramasinghe, editor.

Full Steam Ahead

Alexander Hardison

The sun pours over my body as I streak low over the desert. I bank into a graceful turn, parting steel and bone so tentacles stream behind me. I'm charged up, black steel gleaming over grey flesh, body humming and strong.

"Come on Maze. Time to make a plan." The voice belongs to Cameron. My human partner, my sometime pilot. "Maze? I know you can hear me."

I want to laze here, sun-drunk and happy, not talk about serious things. "Yes, Mother. I promise I'll clean my room and do all my chores."

"You are the room," she says, words curling through an exasperated smile. "You're the chore as well." I can see her through my cameras, gazing down through a viewing blister at a flock of sand kestrels, dark curls tousled over her face.

That makes me laugh. There's no sound—I don't have the lungs or throat for it—but my mind lights up in the way I imagine a human's must when they're amused. For a while, when that happened I'd play the sound of Cameron's laugh through my speakers, but she asked me to stop. Apparently, it's "creepy".

I shift my gelatinous body, reshaping my tail section for speed, and fire the engines strapped to my underbelly. Blue flame joins the void-matter that propels me through the sky. Sandy dunes roll past beneath us, the spires of Norrington glimmering in the east. The distant city is haloed by the radar pings of skyliners, cruise ships and the sleek, beautiful needleships that keep raiders at bay. Traditional vessels, with hulls of complex alloys and crews numbering in the dozens. I describe a lazy turn, putting the city behind us and burning toward our destination, full steam ahead.

I don't really understand that expression. Cameron picked it up from a waterlogged magazine she found back in Junktown, and I always liked how it sounded. We were kids then, small enough for her to ride on my back, undernourished fingers hanging onto my carapace as her bright voice urged me on. She'd point ahead and shout *full steam ahead* as I scrambled down piles of trash, hunting for food and shelter. Our world was a tiny, fearful place, one we had no way of understanding. All we had was each other.

"So," I say. "The plan."

"Yeah. The whale-riders have answered my hails, we'll be there pretty soon. Assuming they want what we've scrounged up, I think I've got the shopping list down to something realistic. Oil and coolant for you, nutrient cakes for me. Maybe some spare parts if we can swing it. Your B and C couplers are showing some wear."

"Shame we can't go back to the manufacturer."

Cameron laughs hollowly. "Yeah. If only." My mechanical parts were built by a dozen different teams; designers and mechanics and madmen, scattered across the continent. Each piece is a totem, a chapter of our journey made manifest. It took years for me to become what I am today, pieced together across the length of our journey.

A line of three great whales drifts into view, dark silhouettes drifting past the rising sun. Their bodies are edged in cilia that scoop up small birds and other airborne critters. The whales are enormous, broad enough for the riders to live in small buildings dotted across their backs. Doors open as we approach, tiny figures gathering along the edges of their world.

I drift above them, fretful and reluctant to descend. "You don't have to do this," I say.

"Do you have a better plan?"

Of course I don't. I just want to keep her safe. She's so tiny, compared to me. Every time she steps outside my body could be the time the world rends her apart. "What if we talked to them by radio, then used the winch when they take the deal? Wouldn't that be easier?"

"The whale-riders take offence easily. You have to look them in the eye if you want to trade." She sighs, frustration creeping into her tone. "Don't you trust me?"

"Of course I do! But last time we tried this they opened fire!"

I feel the warm pressure of her palm on one of my walls. I imagine her there, her solid body zipped into her flight suit, bare palm pressed against my warm, red flesh. "That was a misunderstanding. I'll be okay. I promise."

It's not the riders' fault I look like the voidbeasts that razed their last settlement. I'm not like the rest of my kind, though you wouldn't know if from looking at me. My carapace is pitted and scored, my undercarriage a slimy expanse of flickering, inky tentacles. Cameron found me, abandoned as an infant in Junktown, as helpless and lonely as she was. She saved me from that life, but she can't make me something I'm not.

Don't get me wrong, I love being me, I love the things I can do. But sometimes I look at the Norrington skyliners, and I ache for a life we'll never know. It's not the technicians and engineers, qualified to perform repairs at the drop of a combustion inhibitor, nor the welcome they'd receive at any port. It's the quarters. I've seen the schematics. I know how their crews live. Heated rooms, running water, gymnasiums and cafeterias. Cameron sleeps on a mattress on the floor, under lamps bolted to my soft, red walls. She's installed a few comforts—a food processor, a waste recycler—but my bowels are no kind of home.

"Just think," I say, trying to sound light hearted, "if I were a real ship you'd have showered before your big meeting."

"Mm. That doesn't sound half bad." Her fingers trail downward, tracing the ridges and whorls of my skin. "But would the shower love me?"

I summon my courage and drift lower, close enough for the whale-riders to spot us. "That's my girl," Cameron murmurs, stroking my wall. Apparently, humans always use female pronouns for their ships. The idea doesn't make much sense to me, but it makes Cameron happy.

"I'll have my eyes on you the whole time," I say, trying to sound tough.

"You don't have eyes."

"Oh really? Well then I guess you're fucked, wise guy."

Her ragged chuckle dies too soon. "I'm counting on you."

"If they hurt one hair, I'll ram them out of the sky."

"Be serious, okay?"

"Yeah. Sure." I wasn't joking.

"Okay, bring us down. Give me an hour, then come back around."

"Yes, ma'am." I started calling her that during operations, almost as a joke, addressing her the way the barely sentient warships do their captains. Somewhere along the way, we both started to like it. There's a safety in formality.

The hatch irises open and extends a ropy tendril. Cameron descends the knotted length and sets her feet on the whale's back. I drift higher in the air, giving her space to do what she needs to.

Figures swarm out and encircle her. I hover like an anxious parent, senses straining for any sign of aggression. It's me they hate, but humans are unpredictable things, and it's not beyond them to direct their violence at whatever target comes to hand. I watch her gesture toward me, no doubt indicating the supplies we have to trade. Seedlings from the Archipelago, combustion inhibitors from Golgotha Peak. If we could reach Norrington before our supplies ran out, we could get a good price; instead we'll have to take whatever the riders offer. I hover, frustrated by my helplessness, our lives in the hands of people who hate me for what I am.

—

Eventually Cameron comes back aboard, her face pinched. "Good news, I hope?"

I wait impatiently while Cameron gets a pouch and sucks the water from it. The whales favour salty, fast-moving airstreams—something about the way they breathe—and visiting them leaves her parched. "They took the deal. It'll take a few hours to get the stuff together. We can dock under the lead whale and they'll load us from there."

"That's good news, right? You don't look happy."

"Yeah. I don't know. It's probably nothing. I could tell some of them don't want us there, but they still agreed. Way too easily, actually." She takes another gulp of water. "Maybe I'm being paranoid."

"Paranoia keeps us alive."

"Well, food and oil keeps us alive too."

"Should we still head in?"

She shrugs helplessly. "They've got us over a barrel." Another strange expression, one Cameron won't explain. She jokes that I'm not old enough. We're both about thirty, give or take, but she claims void-beasts live longer than humans so she's the adult. "Take us in."

"Yes, ma'am," I respond, manoeuvring toward the network of straps and rigging that hangs beneath the lead whale. The titanic beast rumbles quietly as I approach, watching me with one still brown eye. They're non-sentient, content to circle the globe in search of food and unmindful of the people settled on their backs. I can't help but wonder for a moment if Cameron would prefer a vessel that didn't snap and sass at every plan.

I settle into the harness, powering down my engines. Cameron's still pacing, hands tight behind her back. Not for the first time, I want to hold her. I see it all the time in trids, human lovers nestled together, arms wrapped achingly tight around each other. I tried to tell her how I felt once, and she only laughed. *You're always holding me*, she said.

"So, what do you want to—"

Bright light. Burning pain. Fire against my flesh. Air rushing past. Whales disappearing into the sky. Falling. I'm falling. Cameron is screaming. Scorching on my carapace. Weapon fire? Explosion? No time. Metal sheeting ripping away. Exposed flesh. I'm spinning, the horizon whipping past. Norrington is a silver streak, a rim on the bowl of the world.

I detonate a canister strapped to my nose. A neutron pulse engulfs us. It's a wild, dangerous move, only slightly less likely to kill us than the onrushing ground. The pulse touches the visible spectrum as a halo of purple and green, surrounding my body in a causality-free bubble. One of the mechanisms ripped away by the blast was the safety interrupt. Energy pours out, draining me in one long burst. We freeze in place, metal fragments glittering in the air around us.

"Maze! Are you there? Come on, you big brat, talk to me."

Time is a strange thing in the bubble. It's been almost a minute already. I let it collapse, metal fragments tumbling to the ground. I power my engines, enough to keep us aloft. "I'm here. What the fuck was that?"

"A bomb, I think. When I said some of them didn't want us there ... I think maybe they *really* didn't want us." Her warm back settles against my walls, swelling as she takes slow, calming breaths. "I'm sorry, this is my fault. I should have known they were up to something."

"Don't be ridiculous. You didn't know. And we're fine. A bit banged up, but nothing your favourite void-extruded abomination can't handle." Both engines suddenly falter, and I go into freefall before shifting around and catching myself. "I think— I think I'm okay."

I'm not. I've taken hits from conventional weaponry before, suffered blasts a dozen times larger than whatever dislodged us from the whales, and none of them felt like this. A wet, sickly pain has soaked into my joints. My body is weak, almost insubstantial, as though the wind were whipping straight through me.

I kick my engines into gear, and the air fills with a terrifying rattling sound. They're strong enough to propel us forward, though not at my usual speed. Still I burn, putting as much distance between us and the whales as possible, in case they decide to finish the job.

"So, now what? Norrington, I guess? It'll be tight, we'll both have to cut down, but we can make it in a few days and we'll be good from there."

"Actually, I think . . ." For the second time in as many minutes, I don't get to finish my sentence. An ice-cold pain pierces my body, and both engines flicker out. I'm falling again, body tumbling toward the desert. Cameron's body crashes to the ground. I reach out, my body moving faster than my mind. Thick, black tentacles tear through their safety braces and lash toward the ground. Voidmatter channels through them, pulsing against the sand, the heat searing it into glass. Steel and titanium riggings tumble away. We stay aloft, held by my natural energy field until the engines come back online.

"Okay," I say shakily. "I think we might be in trouble."

—

Cameron scrambles through my access hatches, the soft pressure of her body slithering through mine in a strange, desperate intimacy. I go over the possibilities as she does—decay in the manifold array, shunting of the taurean cores—but it really doesn't matter. There are less than half a dozen people in the world who understand my inner workings, and I'm not one of them. It never seemed important to learn. There was always another horizon to chase, another adventure to take Cameron on.

My early years are a blur, and I don't know how I got separated from the voidbeast herd. By the time I was making real memories, Cameron was there with me. She was the one who looked after me in Junktown, who named me and taught me human words. We had our own language of gestures and grunts, a strange patois all our own. When we escaped into the real world, she was the one who found the scientists and engineers that worked on me, giving me skin of steel and engines of flame. My best friend, my captain, my midwife.

"So, what's the verdict?" I ask, unsure that I want the answer.

"That pulse took a lot out of you. Your voidmatter interlacing has been atrophying for a while." *Like I tried to tell you*, she doesn't say, but I hear it in her tone.

"I like using the engines. They're faster and easier and they make a cool whooshing sound."

"Well, we're going to be relying on them for the foreseeable. I doubt you could fly under your own power without a lot of rehab. Except . . ."

"Except my engines won't work much longer, either."

"Yeah. Whatever that bomb did to you, the interface between you and the mechanicals is breaking down. Weak, and getting weaker." Cameron slides back into her workroom. Protective gear hits the ground and fingers clatter over keys. I don't have any cameras in there, but I can picture her hunched at the workstation, bathed in the glow of the monitor.

"Why would they do this? And how? I've never felt anything like it."

"Fear? They've been attacked by voidbeasts before. I know, not by us, but maybe if they show they can take one out then the others will stay away. Maybe that's worth getting something special. I've heard there are weaponsmiths who specialise in taking us down."

Taking me down, I think. We've always been a team, but now I'm putting her life in danger. "So, we burn for Norrington, right?"

"The Airborne Academics have gone south for the summer. The Skunkworks have their hands full. We don't have much choice."

"And if the riders come after us, maybe the needleships will intervene."

"Maybe." Her shirt hem crinkles as she fidgets with it, then smoothes it down decisively. "We'll be fine. It'll be tight, I'll be hungry, but this isn't how we die."

It's definitely not how she dies. I'll get her to safety. The desert is harsh, and she's no survivalist. If I crash here, her chances are slim. The closer I get to civilisation before I go down, the better her odds.

I kick into higher gear, turning my nose east. Whatever Cameron's been doing, the motion is a little smoother than before. There's some drift in steering, but I can compensate. I streak low over the desert, close enough to see my shadow dance across the dunes. After a while, greasy black smoke begins to plume behind me. I try not to think about it. Manoeuvring is more difficult at this elevation, but if I drop out of the sky, Cameron might survive. At least, she would if she'd stay in her safety harness. Instead she's scrambling inside me, securing ballast and manually cranking the injectors. "How does that feel?" she for the third time in an hour. "Any better?"

"Yeah, much better. Thank you." I'm lying, but it's what she needs to hear. If she doesn't stay busy, panic will set in.

"What else can I do? Do you need more coolant?"

"It's fine. You should get some sleep. You'll save energy."

"Yeah. Yeah, that's a good idea." She sits on a crate and sighs, making no move toward her bed. "Do you ever think about Arcadia?"

"Yeah." I wait for her to go on, but she doesn't. "Why do you ask?"

There's a warm pressure against my wall. I picture her on a crate, knees tucked against her body, chin on grease-streaked hands. "I woke up this morning, and for the longest moment, I thought I was back there. I knew, right down in my bones, that when I opened my eyes I'd see metal figures all around my bunk. The little river running past, you out there collecting firewood or working on the shelter. The sun coming up over the mountains, making everything shimmer and glow."

"Gods, you worked so hard on those figures." I don't forget things, not like humans do, but I can set memories aside for a while. Arcadia is something I haven't thought about for a long time. Nostalgia rushes over me, briefly displacing the fear and pain. I was smaller then, larger than Cameron but not yet at my full size, perambulating around on a mass of thick black tentacles. I see Cameron, clambering back into our little home base, arms laden with curious pieces of metal and wood. She'd sit in the dirt, bare feet splayed to either side, twisting and combining them with quick, clever movements. We were there for months, long enough for a tiny menagerie to spring up around us. We did the necessary work of survival, hunting and building and watching for predators, but all the while she built her tiny figures. A miniature settlement, full of silent friends. She even made a little sign, the name taken from an old-world poem. Arcadia. It was our first home together, and in many ways the best. Arcadia was where we learned to communicate; years before the Airborne Academics wired speakers into my brainstem, she and I sat on the ridge, miming out words with my slimy tentacles and her dirty little hands.

Cameron doesn't say anything. She doesn't need to explain why she brought it up. Arcadia has always been a shorthand for failure. For the moment I woke up with a terrified lurch, rain on my body, water halfway up my carapace. I was supposed to be on watch. I was supposed to be looking after our little home. Instead I'd slept, the rains came in, and Arcadia was gone.

Cameron makes all sorts of excuses for me. I hadn't slept for days. I was still poisoned and weak from an animal attack the night before. None of that brings back Arcadia. The river swelled and we lost it all; food and gear and everything Cameron had worked to build. She splashed though icy black water, body shaking with desperate tears, pulling out scraps of her menagerie until I caught her by the armpits and lifted her out. Nothing could be saved.

I'm not letting her down again.

—

Cameron finally sleeps. Usually I miss her while she's in her bunk, but right now I have too much to plan. I've already calculated how far I can get on my fuel reserves, the optimal course and speed factored against our dwindling supplies. There are moments when I'm as strong as I've ever been, and there are those when I'm certain the ground is about to rush up and claim me. I crunch the numbers over and over, trying to see what I've missed, trying to find the outcome where we both survive.

A stab of pain. Deeper this time, like a blade sliding up into my gut. It's like that scene in *Archibald Equinox*, the one at the end of every episode, where he and the villain both draw their blades and rush at each other, but Equinox is always quicker, darting close and driving his weapon up into the evil-doer's guts. I hate that show, so predictable, but Cameron can't get enough. We have a little projector set up in one of my chambers, with a couch and a camera so we can watch together. She says it's nice, the way things always work out, even if the mysteries get really silly after the third season, and I don't like how they recast the evil magistrate after the fifth . . .

It's getting hard to focus. The point is that it hurts. I don't have the luxury of overthinking any longer. Any moment now, my engines will die and I'll fall from the sky. If not that, then my steering ailerons will jam, or my nacelles will get blocked, or any number of irreparable faults. They play out in my mind, distinct at first, then blurring together into a kaleidoscope of failure and death. I lurch to the side and Cameron scrambles to her feet.

"Talk to me Maze. What's happening?"

I try to say something, but the words don't come out right. There's another stab of pain, and we lurch lower. I correct, hauling us painfully back into the sky. Cameron's ragged breath is deafening. I've used up all my tricks. All I have left is bloody-mindedness. I discard the calculations and accelerate, pointing my nose at Norrington and burning as hard as I can. My housings rattle, steel heating and singeing the flesh beneath. I don't care. I have to move.

"It's over, Maze," Cameron says, her voice tight with resignation. When I don't respond she pounds her fist against my wall. "Fucking hell, Maze, land! You're going to kill yourself, you stubborn bitch."

It's hard to find words, harder still to set them in the right order. "Not. Letting you. Down."

"You're going to crash! Then we both die! You think that doesn't count?"

I'm not listening. I have my eyes on Norrington. It's not getting any closer. I burn harder and faster. I'll get there in the end. Cameron will be safe.

Footfalls inside me, spaced out like she's running. Muttered curses. Metal slides painfully over flesh, and then there's an empty looseness I've not felt before. Air rushes over flesh that hasn't felt it in years. I don't understand what's happening, and I don't have the words to ask.

Another sharp shock, lower down this time. Steel ribbing tumbles to the ground behind me. Confusion wars with betrayal. Cameron is tearing me apart.

I put on a burst of speed, trying to outrun whatever madness has seized her. There's a loud retort, and my whole body shakes. One of the engines is loose in its housing, spluttering wildly. If I don't set down soon, I'm going to spin out of control. Still, I lay on the speed, dunes racing past below us, black smoke streaming behind. Another shudder, and part of my steering mechanism tumbles to the ground.

"Please, Maze," Cameron says, more exhausted than afraid. "You can't go on now. When I throw this next bolt you'll be crippled. Don't make me. Please, don't make me do it. Land. Somewhere, anywhere. Land and let us sort out what happens next."

"If I land, I'm not getting back up. If I stop flying now, then we'll never fly together again, and flying with you is the only thing that matters."

"Do you trust me?"

My mind spins, the pain so deep that I no longer know who I'd be without it.

"Do you trust me?" She's shouting, her words strangled and wet. "You don't have to save me, Maze. We're a team. You have to talk to me, we have to work together, and you have to fucking trust me!"

I think of her lost in the desert, dying alone, her bones bleaching under the sun. All my fault.

"I trust you with my life every single day, Maze. Why can't you trust me?"

I do trust her. But the thought of her being hurt is overwhelming. I say nothing. My seams are burning, loose metal joins rattling over abraded flesh.

Cameron slumps to the ground. I feel it like part of my body dying. "Do you know why I brought up Arcadia before?" she asks, her voice strangely quiet.

"Because I failed you."

"No! Gods, Maze, no. I've told you this a thousand times. You didn't fail me." She runs her hand through her hair, gathering her thoughts. "I mentioned Arcadia because it was the end of that part of our lives. We'd been camped there for so long. Too long. The dogs were getting bolder, and we both suspected the water runoff was making me sick. We had to go, we just didn't want to admit it."

I don't say anything. I can't think about are her little figures, the ones she worked so hard on, swept away by the rush of black water. Her wet, frightened sobs as we struggled away from the little home we'd made together.

"That was the end of that part of our lives. And it hurt. We mourned. And then we kept going. Full steam ahead. And do you remember what happened a few days later?"

"I learned to fly."

"That's right," Cameron breathes as the dunes surge up to meet us. "Don't you want to see what comes next?"

"I do. Gods, yes, I do. I trust you. I love you." I steady myself as much as I can. "Do it."

There's a heavy clunk, and a sudden looseness in my tail section. Both engines fall away. We hurtle in silence, a ballistic mass containing the most beautiful girl in the world. I clench my body tight, watching the dunes rise to meet us.

Then I'm firing my braking jets, slowing our descent as much as I can. We split through the top of the first dune and bounce into the air, spinning wildly. I try to compensate, my telemetry hasty and imprecise. We hit the next one, sliding down the bank, the last of my rigging tearing away. My external sensors are ripped away. I'm blind. When we come to rest my body is almost entirely bare, racked with pain and ragged with abrasion.

"Cameron?" No answer. My internal views are dead. "Cameron?" I can't feel her moving inside me. Can't feel anything. I twitch on the spot, trying to move, tentacles thrashing helplessly at the sand. I can already tell I'll never fly again. I'm wounded and helpless and alone. Cameron is dead inside me, crushed by crates or slammed against a wall. I don't know how long it'll take me to follow. Too long.

A few days after Arcadia was swept away, we made a little camp behind a bulwark of stained mattresses and metal sheeting. Our bonfire spewed noxious smoke, but it was better than the cold. Cameron had been sick for a long time. I was still in shock from the loss of our home. All I knew was that we had to keep moving. There had to be somewhere better than this. Someplace safe, where the air didn't taste like oil and grit.

We fell asleep in the usual way: Cameron curled against me, my carapace open to the fire's warmth. My body was fat and bulbous, longer than hers by far. I woke in a state of complete disorientation. The fire was gone. The shelter was gone. The nearby cliff was replaced by a thin white line some distance below me.

There was the strangest feeling inside me, like one of my organs was crashing around in a panic. I tried to leap up, and suddenly I was airborne, propelled by voidmatter flowing through my body. Cameron's screams filled my senses and the ground fell away. It was a long time before we understood what was happening, and longer still before I learned to control my new form. Eventually we found a way to make it work, discovered the pockets inside me where Cameron could survive and the techniques to keep me airborne. I grew larger still, but by then we were on our way, leaving Junktown in search of a better life. Full steam ahead.

With my metal frame removed, the sickly pain of my injury subsides. Into its absence floods the flat nausea of despair. The desert wind whips eddies of sand across my body. The sun is warm, almost pleasantly so, as it drifts toward the horizon. Norrington is a silver glow in the distance. I'll never reach it now. This will be my whole world, for the rest of my days.

Movement, somewhere inside my body. A shifting, like debris settling into place after the crash. It must be. It couldn't be Cameron. I won't allow myself to hope. The movement stops, but I find my senses straining, desperate beyond measure. The only movement is the wind.

There's a tiny grunt, and I feel my leeward hatch pop open. Cameron climbs out, battered but alive. Unsteady footsteps move down my side. I want to scream in relief. I want to cry.

My despair broken, I prise open my eyes. My organic ones. They're weak and imprecise, and the effort makes them ache, but it's worth it to see Cameron. She's resting at my side, nursing an injured arm but upright and alive. We've fetched up near a cluster of small brown trees, and beyond them glimmers a pool of water. Further away, but moving toward us, I hear the putter and whine of land vehicles, approaching. Mercenaries, perhaps, or traders. Cameron pulls her cloak around herself and pats my flank. "We're going to be okay," she murmurs. I know that look. She's making plans, calculating what comes next. It takes me a moment to recognise the look on her face. It's hope. As the future tumbles down the dunes toward us, I let myself feel the same.

Truth Be Told

Louise Pieper

His ripe sweat sours over carbolic soap, all glazed in guilt and dust and despair. I catch the stranger's scent as he crosses the footbridge from what's left of the village. It stills my pacing and draws me to the door where I wait in the shadows. The old woman's skin wraps about me, clinging like the caress of a drowned man. The stranger steps past the trees and I shake my head.

The weather is wrong.

It's a drowsy afternoon at the end of a long, hot summer and he is a creature meant for winter's cold austerity. Beneath the slouch hat and the dirt of travel, his face is frost set, sharp-boned and riven by a wide, thin mouth. Home is the soldier boy, home from the war, but home is not as he left it. Invisible in the dark fortress of the hut, I let myself smile.

He will do.

Not that I'm hungry. Yet. The old woman's bitter lies, bounteous from decades of vicious deceptions, will sustain me for weeks more although the river was in spring spate when I came up from it, drawn by the scent of her vileness. This broken toy soldier is too young to provide a feast such as the hag. Still, he followed the drum and fed the crows.

All killers are liars.

He stops at the gate and fear flickers across his face. What does he see? The hut slumps; resigned to decay. Its rough timber slabs are silvered and spotted with lichen and it sags like a rock-snarled shipwreck. Hessian-bleary windows squint at the river. Weeds have conquered the roof's shingles, generals whose offspring besiege the yard.

"Missus?" he calls and raises one hand against the westering sun. "Uh . . . Annis?"

The skin shivers at its name.

"Who wants to know?" I rasp.

Four moons of solitude turn my words harsh as crows squabbling over carrion.

"It's . . ."

He pauses, wets his lips and I lick mine, ready to taste his first lie.

"I'm one of the baker's boys."

Truth.

"I went . . . There's no-one . . ."

I step through the doorway and let him see this old skin. I'm stooped to fit its constriction and draped in the shapeless layers of the hag's hodden homespun.

"You went away soldiering," I say, because that's plain as a pikestaff. "Joined the army to help win the war."

"They said we won," he agrees. "But . . ."

"Aye, but. How many years gone?" I ask, although the hag would know.

"Five," he says. "Almost five."

His words have the crisp bite of truth, sharp as the cider apples growing up by the old mill, the ones the skin remembers.

"Drought." I shrug. "Famine. Fire and pestilence."

Each word wounds, a sabre slash to his hopes. I glance east, where the distant smoke of pillage has been rising into the hot, blue sky since noon.

"Predators."

I don't add I'm one of them, nor that the lying hag whose skin I wear had picked clean the bones of the children who survived the plague, long before the river brought me to her.

"For true," I say, "you were so busy with War, you forgot the other Horsemen."

"They said we won," he repeats, voice breaking, hopes shattering, all that kept him going through years of pain and death tearing apart and scattering to the dirt.

"They lied." I turn for the door.

"Please," he cries.

His grief-honest pain catches me, tearing at my stolen skin. It hurts.

"Please, Annis. I have nowhere to go."

Not true, it's not true—there is the whole, wide world, everywhere, anywhere but here—yet it chimes like a bell, truth giving tongue to the brass in a ringing peal.

"Can I stay?"

"Are you not afraid?" I ask and though I use a stolen voice, I let a little of what I am slide out to scare him off or force a lie, because I am the one who casts the hooks. I am the Great of Death, the Eater of Hearts who feeds on their falsehoods. I am the Doom and the Devourer.

They do not make me *feel*.

"Afraid? Gods, yes," he says, a truth as large as the sky. "What I believed of you when I was a child." He shudders and grips the gatepost with one hand. "Our parents told us if we were not good Old Annis would eat us. I'm terrified, but . . ."

He raises his gaze to mine and my head whirls with the force of his truth.

"I would make a tough meal, now, and I'm more afraid of being alone."

I want to strike him, rend him, devour him for daring to flaunt his brutal honesty. What sort of soldier boy admits fear to an old woman? What man has ever chosen my company over the safety of solitude? What stupid, frail, fallible, lying human has ever, ever heaped my plate with so much pain-sweet truth?

"What do I call you?" I growl.

"Birch," he says.

"Billy Birch the baker's boy," I say, catching a wet-lipped, wish-plump echo from the skin.

"Just Birch," he insists. "I lost Billy somewhere in the trenches."

Truth.

"You can stay in the woodshed," I snarl.

Then I stalk into the hut and slam the door.

—

I cast off clothes and skin and I rage. I lash my tail and snap my jaws. I stomp from the bed, laden with human husks, to the wall against which the woodshed leans. I punish him for that truth-soaked pain, deny him the company he craves and think him well-served for his presumption. I tell myself it will be all the sweeter when I feed on his lies and steal his skin.

He moves about, eats and settles.

I lean against the wood, angry at his scent, at the weight of his presence beyond the hut's thin wall. He sighs, puppy-soft and vulnerable, and matches his breathing to mine. I gasp and deny him that crutch. His breath catches and he moans, cries out a name. I press against the wood, breathless. Let him wake and be afraid. Let him wake and quit this accursed place.

Let him wake.

He cries and thrashes, kicking against the weight of memory, fighting the past. *He had a bad war*, I've heard men say, as if there's any other kind. Another name is wrenched from him—a stillborn word, clotted with the memory of old blood, drenched in pain.

Why doesn't he wake?

Another name. He screams denial. It's not true, but a terrible sort of truth. In that moment, he'd unmake the world if it would change what happened. I drive my claws into the boards to keep to my feet, staggering as the force of his loss rushes through me like a flood. My ears ring with it and it's some time before I hear his weeping.

"Birch," I croak through the boards, forcing the sound through a throat not designed for human speech. Louder, above his sobs. "Birch!"

He mumbles something, another name or perhaps a rank.

"You're safe enough," I growl. "Go back to sleep."

"Safe?" he murmurs, throat raw, sleep-drunk and trusting as a fresh-licked cub.

"Safe," I say. "For now. For true."

"Annis." He says the skin's name like a benediction.

He sighs and shifts. Cloth rustles, joints settle and his breaths lengthen and deepen, sliding him back into restful sleep. I sink onto my haunches beside the wall, flesh-heavy though my head still surges with that agonised deluge, and I breathe with him.

—

The soldier boy works. I watch. More than solitude, he fears inaction and the thoughts which beset him if he's not busy. Always busy with some task. The sun wheels across the sky and he works until it sinks, exhausted with watching him. Day follows day. He tames the weeds, fixes the roof, mends the fences, nurtures the garden, which is sullen at first and then lavish in its bounty as it yields to him.

I scowl at the vegetables and vow not to succumb.

He doesn't lie, although he says he lied about his age when he enlisted. He doesn't wear his honesty like a badge, nor give credit for it to the gods. Can a man forget how to lie? Or have the lies he suffered for exhausted his own store of duplicity?

I don't care.

All killers are liars. Nay, all men are liars. They lie and cheat and kill until the weight of their lies draws my regard and then they lie no more. Bandits and looters, villains of every kind pollute the world. They etch their deeds in smoke on the sky, each day closer to the hut.

They would be easy prey.

He whistles as he planes boards to build a new woodshed. I watch the bunch and slide of muscles revealed by the thin cotton vest he wears. He knows I'm behind him, but he doesn't mind. He's grown comfortable with the hag's skin and I grow tired of waiting.

"I'm going away for a while," I tell him.

He turns, stuttering denial. I shrug and the skin catches cold and foul on the scales of my neck.

"It's not safe," he says, glancing also at the distant smoke.

"One of my . . . someone will come," I say. It's almost a lie. "You won't be alone."

He flushes and drops his gaze to his boots.

"I meant for you," he says. "There are outlaws. Ruthless men. It's not safe."

Truth. Or so he thinks. The skin wants to curl its lip at his concern, but I don't let it. A laugh roars out of me instead.

"I'm safe enough," I say.

———

I return late the next day, stump-heavy in the man-skin.

Birch chops timber, filling the new woodshed. He breaks off when he sees me, gaze wary, and raises the axe between us. I'm not surprised. The skin is ugly and hulking, easy to wear, but no-one trusts it. I force the lips into a smile, an expression they won't hold.

"Birch, right?" I grunt and raise my bag. "Want a drink?"

His winter-cold face takes on an extra rime of frost.

"Annis sent you?"

He's still holding the axe like it'd help him if this lumbering skin went for his throat. Maybe it would and all. They can be tricky, humans.

"She didn't send me," I say. "For true, I go where I want."

He swings up the axe and lets it rest easy on his shoulder, but his grip stays firm. His body lies, why doesn't he? Still, only false words let me get my hooks into someone, so I do nothing more than lick the skin's lips and say again, "Drink?"

"What's your name?" he asks. "You know I'm Birch."

"Call me Mutt."

He nods and doesn't say anything.

And that's how it goes. He presses his lips together until they're scar-thin, but he doesn't lie because he doesn't speak. I joke with him, bait him, challenge him—all the foolish things men do that lead them into lies and violence. He just smiles tightly, gaze tracking over the skin like it's a puzzle he can't solve. He refuses a fourth drink and gets to his feet, steady on the other side of the fire-pit.

"I've met men like you before," he says and I let the skin have its sour little chuckle, though he's speaking truth, as far as he knows.

"I don't think so," I say.

He just shrugs and heads for his woodshed and uneasy sleep.

—

I shed the bullying brute's skin and fling it onto the bed. I won't keep it once I have Birch. He's cold, the soldier boy, with a thin mouth and eyes like poisoned wells, but he'll make a better skin than the hulking Mutt. Spare husks are easily found. Liars let me under their skin. The first hook goes in with the first lie. Two lies and they feel it catch, know something's wrong. But they can't help themselves—they lie a third time and they are mine.

I pick up another skin.

He didn't lie to the hag. He didn't lie to the brute. He would lie to the bawd.

—

Submerged, only my eyes and nostrils break the surface. I drift and soak in the river's gossip—all it has seen and heard as it tumbles down from the mountains, flows through fields and towns, rumbles under bridges and burbles over fords listening to brigands, murderers, thieves and thugs. The whispered words of faithless lovers, the hollow assurances of corrupt officials, the oily cheer of cutthroats. Liars, so many liars, all easy to take.

And there is Birch, pulling off his boots on the riverbank.

The river's rumours tug at me. Other liars can sate the hollowness that grows within. I can take the skin I've brought and swim away. Leave him to the hag's hut and the hope that others will settle here again. He's put down roots, sure as the plants he's nurtured. But if I'm wrong about him, my winter-dark, broken soldier boy, what else am I wrong about?

No. All men are liars.

I watch him strip shirt, trousers, vest and drawers. He wades into the river, soap-clutching, scarred skin puckering, the scent of Mutt's alcohol lifting from his pores. I slither away while he scrubs his hair. Not that he would see me, if I did not wish to be seen.

The skin lies where I left it, beneath the dog willow.

I shudder as I shake it out, flapping it as laundresses do with the sheets they boil. It would be good to boil away this skin's sour floral musk. I wrap myself in it, feel the slime-slick press, the weight of its greedy lies. I snarl as it settles over me, masking me, moulding me to its hated shape. The skin's dress is a further prison, tucked and boned and seamed to form the silhouette of a man's desire. I can barely breathe and barely walk.

Hip-deep in the water, Birch watches the hut. He doesn't see me totter along the riverbank to where I can pose and say, "Don't wash it off, soldier boy."

I expect him to spin around, blush and bluster. Instead he turns slowly, hands loose, and he says nothing, only stares.

"Cat got your tongue?" I ask because it's one of the stupid human things this skin would say.

He shudders and says, "What do you want?"

I thrust out my chest and drop one hip, a move that's second nature to this skin. I let my hunger peep through in my gaze, but I bite off the answer the skin would give, because it would be a lie.

Suddenly, I am furious with myself.

I skirt lies and play with the truth. I set traps before him with my skins, to drink or seduce him into deceit so I can devour him. There's no need for such lures and tactics when the river told me of liars who boast of their deceptions. I should have swum away.

A growl rises in my chest.

He jerks his head around to stare toward the village, then charges out of the water at me. He's all wet, soft-slapping pale skin, scar-puckered down one side like a half-melted wax poppet. I put up one hand, thinking to hold him off, but he stops to grab his boots and shove his muddy feet into them.

"Come on," he urges and before I can think what to say, the wind shifts, and I smell them.

Four men, smoke-seeped with old blood on their blades. Villains on the bridge.

Birch snatches up his shirt and ties it around his hips, covering those parts humans worry about so much. If I wasn't quaffing the bandits' lie-drenched scent I'd laugh to think he'd mind this skin's modesty.

"Come on," he repeats, grasping my elbow.

I stagger a few steps, caught in the villains' reek. He bends and scoops me up, still moving, and it's his turn to stagger as I prove heavier than the skin seems. He catches his stride, though, and runs for the hut with me pressed to his wet chest.

Then I do laugh, because he's saving me, my ridiculous soldier boy gallant. Or so he thinks.

"Put me down, Birch," I say.

"Bandits," he gasps. "They'll hurt you."

"For true, they won't," I growl.

He releases my legs as we round the corner of the hut and his arm around the skin's waist keeps me from staggering. He reaches into the old woodshed and grabs his rifle.

"I can hold them off," he says, watching the gate. "You'll make the orchard if you run."

"Not in this dress," I say.

"Gods, Annis, I don't want them to—"

I grab his throat.

"What did you call me?"

"Annis," he croaks.

Truth.

I shove him into the woodshed and follow him inside. The space is too small to hold him and this skin and my towering rage.

"How did you know?" I hiss.

His face is red, and he claws at my hand, but he doesn't raise the rifle, so I let go and repeat, "How?"

"You–" He coughs. "Your eyes don't change. Annis, Mutt, this lady. Your voice sounds different, but you speak the same. You swear by truth. And you–" He looks at the floor. "You smell the same. Like the reed beds by the river."

Truth.

"Humans can't smell that well," I say, and his colour leaches out as he realises what I admit.

"Knock, knock," a man shouts from the gate. "Is Old Annis still here? We've come to see if you need any help."

I splay my hand over Birch's chest, pinning him against the wall between the shed and the hut. The skin's nostril's quiver as I breathe in the bandit's vinegar-sour, kale-bitter words. My first hook slides under the weight of his deception to lodge deep in the liar's belly.

"Liar," Birch spits.

Truth.

How can he know? I realise I've voiced the thought when he answers.

"It was a mortar." He trembles, gaze turned inwards. "The trench collapsed. They dug me out saying it was alright. But it wasn't. Everyone else . . ." He gasps in a breath. "I touched Death, or it touched me. I can smell things I shouldn't and, when I hear a lie, my mouth tastes of mud and blood again. I can't bear it."

I pat his chest, like he's a clever pup, and he adds, "You don't lie."

"Neither do you." I grin and press fingers to his lips.

"Who is it?" I call, the skin's voice high and wavering.

A coarse laugh and the thud of flesh striking flesh as the villain silences his thugs. Birch's eyes are huge and pleading.

"Just travellers," the bandit shouts. "Friends."

The second hook catches deep in his groin, stilling the itch that the skin's girlish quaver started. He grunts and it runs back through my hooks, making me shiver.

"What are you doing?" Birch mouths against my fingers.

"He lies and gives himself away."

"They'll rape and kill us, ransack this place, torch the hut. I don't care how you've done this–" He flicks his gaze over the skin. "You're honest and you don't deserve to die. If I draw their fire, can you get away?"

"You sound too nice to be Old Annis." The voice wheedles, greased by visions of the violence to come. "What's your name, sweetheart?"

I raise the skin's voice, sweet and hesitant. "Some folk call me Amie."

"Annis is dead," I growl to Birch. "She lied and I killed her. I kill liars."

Birch slumps against the wall, all the tension draining out of him, his winter-bleak eyes leaking tears.

"I thought I'd have to do it. Stop the liars. Kill them. Why else can I taste lies? And I don't . . . I can't . . ." He hefts the rifle, hand shaking, and I push it down.

"I can." My smile grows wide, wider than this skin can contain. It splits and drops to the ground. "That's what I'm here for."

"Gods." Birch stares at me: at my hide, scales and fur; my claws and jaws, my dozens of dagger-sharp, lie-devouring teeth. Great of Death. Devourer. "Dear gods."

Truth.

"Come out, come out," the villain yells, like a fairy-tale wolf at the door. "We won't hurt you, sweetheart."

The third hook buries itself deep in the bandit's throat. I smile at Birch and warily, wonderingly, he smiles back. Then I step out of the woodshed and tug the liar's leaden soul from his skin.

Transcendence Inc.

C.H. Pearce

"Thrifty," called Vangelis.

Thrift lifted his head. He was slumped at the kitchen counter, curled protectively around a glass of scotch.

Vangelis only called him *Thrifty* when he wanted something, which was always. Sounding out of breath, Vangelis clicked the apartment door shut behind him. He rarely emerged from the labs at lunchtime to idle with Thrift in the apartment above the Transcendence complex. It was accessible only via the fire stairs.

"Do you know anyone, Thrifty, who'd like to be my first volunteer?" Vangelis worried at the neck of his t-shirt, as if wishing it had a collar with buttons and a tie he might loosen, like Thrift's. He was sweating, despite the air-conditioning.

Thrift worked in entertainment. He knew plenty of people who wanted to live forever. But he heard a tap-tap-tapping on the window and turned his head.

The apartment was three storeys up. The living room window was a narrow strip of glass. Through it, Thrift could just make out the heat-shimmer above the railing of an empty balcony. The haze was too thick to see as far as the New Sydney shore.

Thrift was momentarily startled to see a large, white bird hovering on the other side of the glass. A real bird? Outside, in this heat? He slid off the barstool and advanced on it suspiciously, pressed his long-fingered hands to the glass. Found it hot to the touch.

It was a delivery drone, hovering like an overlarge hummingbird, staring into the apartment with beady, black eyes. It settled on the balcony railing. In its beak it gripped a white plastic delivery bag, like a stork presenting a human baby.

Thrift hated that delivery bird.

"You ordered CleanEats?" Thrift called back over his shoulder.

Thrift slid open the door to the balcony when Vangelis nodded. He had an exceptional tolerance for heat, and it was understood he always volunteered to take deliveries.

A blast of hot air struck Thrift when he stepped outside. He closed the door behind him.

The stork swivelled its head, and shone a beam of red light into Thrift's eyes. "You're not Dr Eli Vangelis. What are you? Eyes open. Stand up straight. Sir, you're moving . . ."

Thrift recoiled, cursing. He batted the stork away. While it was recovering its bag, he brandished his mobile. "Scan my phone."

The stork hesitated. "Not CleanEats Inc.'s preferred mode of identification. Organic verification is preferred. I —I mean *we* —like eyes."

"Eyes?" demanded Thrift sharply. The stork was alarmingly off script. Worse, it spoke in his own voice—unsurprising, as Thrift had done the audio—but he'd exclusively used a mellifluous bass voice, modelled after a self-styled preacher Thrift had known in the cult. And yet here it was, displaying *range*.

"You might have stolen someone else's external device." The stork persisted. "And made them give you the code."

"For a takeaway lunch order?"

The stork scanned the phone. It turned its head away, the carry bag sliding in its beak. In amplified imitation of Thrift's own voice, it intoned: "Leave the empty containers for collection tomorrow morning."

It beeped once, pleasantly, and flew away.

Thrift, left clutching the bag, shuddered. He should never have let CleanEats take more than audio to assist with the autocomplete.

Thrift looked out over the railing until the heat crept through the soles of his shoes. Waves washed over the sandbar and slapped against the wharf of the manmade island. The water was pink-tinged and slightly foamy, like spit in a dentist's cup after a tooth extraction.

When Thrift returned, Vangelis meticulously divided the microburgers and cold brew. Each burger was the size of a thumbnail.

"You'd be my first choice for testing, Thrifty. But you already told me no."

"*I'll only break the system.*" Thrift put on his most sinister bass voice. He'd cut his teeth on bit-part villains. The sort who were credited as Henchman #2 and died ten minutes in. "Test on real people, not actors. Once we're getting regular clients into your virtual heaven you can turn that brain of yours to sneaking this unsuitable one in."

Thrift was a human impersonator, and a competent enough one to have everyone fooled, so far. Every night he crashed into bed exhausted from the effort. Playing villains was a snap. Demons were second-nature. The exception to the act was Vangelis, who he'd known since his first confused attempts to fit in at their local primary school after child services pulled him from the cult of the New Beelzebub. Post-apocalypse cults proliferated after the decisive climate events of the mid-2000s, and the subsequent scrapping over what was left.

Vangelis frequently suggested therapy.

"Eventually, if you want to Transcend to a virtual heaven, you're going to have to overcome this odd conviction you're a demon." Vangelis laughed.

Vangelis was the real thing. Vangelis wore black under his lab coat;

sported a goatee; had, in their startup, a lair. A trinity of crimes. He wore socks and sandals and tucked his trousers into his socks. There was nothing Thrift could say about that.

"You're going to have to overcome your conviction," said Thrift, "that I'm not. It's too late, anyway. We signed the contract. In blood."

"I'm unconvinced the blood was necessary."

"You'll figure it out. I'll get you money, and a volunteer."

Thrift picked up a microburger between a long white forefinger and thumb, squeezing it, examining it for imperfections. "Do you want someone I like, or someone I don't like?"

"Someone you like," said Vangelis accusingly.

The microburger looked perfect to Thrift. He ate it in one gulp on his way downstairs. It tasted like paper.

—

Mr Grot Bowerdust shook hands with Thrift heartily in his new office, and drew him in for a back-slap, as if he hadn't six months ago reneged on Thrift's three-film contract and stopped answering his vidcalls. Bowerdust had moved on to Immersifilm.

The Immersifilm office was difficult to find in the pea-soup haze of Old Sydney. Thrift sweated through his thin shirt on the short walk from car to stairwell.

After the handshake, Bowerdust flicked his hand absently and wiped it on his trouser-leg. But he beamed at Thrift. His incongruous response was typical. Thrift was arresting in audio; rakish in vid; in person, oily and unsettling, with a handshake like a damp eel. All slicked-back hair and long pale limbs and a well-tailored suit that stank of sweat and smoke, as if he'd walked through fire to get there.

The deal with totally immersive tech was a good one. "You've a good voice, and you still have a nostalgic, alternative sort of appeal," explained Bowerdust. He sat behind his desk, swept aside coffee cups, and invited Thrift to sit as if for an interview.

Thrift lit a cigarette and tried not to look pleased. "Thirty, and not past it? Or is it immersive tech I might, perhaps, adapt to after all?" Thrift had so far been failing to get work in the immersive space. An unnerving deficiency, because immersive looked set to make vid obsolete and he couldn't earn enough for Vangelis doing audio for drones. "Either way, that's good news. What's the role? Can I work from home?"

"Better. Upload yourself as an Immersifilm character, no need to act again. Our techies will cast your faithfully rendered I-copy in a variety of worlds, original and derivative, to be interacted with by paying users in their own homes."

Thrift regarded the I-copy machine with a raised eyebrow. It looked like an airport full-body scanner, sitting incongruously alongside a shredder and an overfull wastepaper basket.

"Very expensive," prompted Bowerdust.

"What are the rules? For user behaviour, possible worlds, the I-copy..."

"What's the appeal of an immersive fantasy realm if it has rules? Anyway, you won't be playing. I-Thrift does the acting from now on, and you get a quarterly payment."

Bowerdust had the contract printed. "Sound good?"

Thrift leafed through, pen poised.

All human originals must pass preliminary test scan to confirm suitability...

"I have to discuss it with my partner." Thrift set down the pen. He felt himself a teenager checking in with his foster mother in front of his fashionable new friends.

"Your business partner? That's Dr Eli Vangelis?" Bowerdust's brows came together in thought. "Not that grim, sour-faced, beardy who hung around at your parties?"

Thrift smiled, nodded.

Bowerdust pressed the contract into Thrift's hands. "I always figured he was your supplier, something like that."

—

That evening, Vangelis threw the contract on the kitchen counter with the old takeaway boxes.

"If you want to keep bleeding me for money," Thrift cautioned, slowly, "don't forbid me from working."

"Not these Immersifilm hacks," insisted Vangelis. "You read the contract? I-Thrift would be a bot. If it acts out, you're legally culpable. It's your reputation..."

"Ergo, your funding." Thrift quietly fixed himself a scotch.

"I'm only looking out for you, Thrifty. Yes—and myself." Vangelis held up a hand. "Our interests are entwined. That's the price of any partnership. I need you alive, and well, and out of jail to fund my research. Because if you don't give me the resources I need, I can't create our virtual heaven, and *sneak* you in. In which case, I understand I'll breach contract, and—" Vangelis hesitated fractionally, put a hand over his mouth. "—see you in hell."

Thrift didn't like how Vangelis faltered when he spoke about hell, not from fear, but from a half-supressed laugh. His lips quirked, too, when he spoke about *sneaking* Thrift in.

"I don't yet fully understand it myself. The cult leaders were unbalanced and they bickered constantly. '*Let's sacrifice the boy*,' '*no, let's use him as a vessel*'..." Thrift alternated between an older-sounding male and female voice. "No grasp of reality, let alone..." He tailed off.

Vangelis rubbed his temples in silent exasperation. Closed his eyes a moment.

Vangelis still did not entirely believe. But neither did he entirely disbelieve. He'd stopped chuckling, briefly, while signing their contract when Thrift handed him a knife.

That was one thing Thrift liked about Vangelis. He was a difficult man to unnerve.

"Stick to your audio and vid, Thrifty. Immersive isn't for you."

Thrift raised an eyebrow. Did he already understand?

" . . .immersive is the future, yes, but no one is utilising it like Transcendence. Immersifilm is a rush job, using insufficiently tested equipment, poorly designed and legally questionable and horrifically small-minded and unambitious. Your I-copy would do something unspeakable to a user who had a private fantasy it didn't like within two minutes. Then you'd be in jail and un-hireable, and I—I'm sorry, *we*— would run out of money, and I won't be able to complete my work for you. Mutual interests. See?"

Thrift nodded. He thought that an uncharacteristically clear explanation. "*Do* you work for me? Or do I work for you? Drink?"

After that it degenerated.

―

Thrift felt his phone in his pocket, and resisted checking the time. Vangelis had been talking for at least twenty minutes.

"You and I are onto the real thing. If you want to create a virtual heaven, it's the world and its rules you have to perfect. When I upload your consciousness to our new world, I'll do it faithfully. It really will be you and your old body will die. That's the part we'll have trouble selling."

"I can sell it." Thrift waved a hand dismissively. "How about I put the containers out for the stork?"

He took the scotch with him. On the balcony, a new bag was waiting.

When he came back Vangelis was still talking. Thrift opened the bag. This wasn't CleanEats.

Inside was a small, square packet. Thrift prodded it. He shuddered, imagining that the stork had plucked out and brought him a customer's eyeball.

"For your bedside lamp," Vangelis prompted. "The bulb went months ago."

"I hadn't noticed," Thrift lied. He had stopped reading in bed at night rather than address it.

"You do know how to change a lightbulb?"

"If I change the bulb," explained Thrift patiently, "it will explode and short everything. Even with the power off."

"That one time, when we were eight? Hardly conclusive. Have you really never changed a lightbulb since?"

Thrift downed his scotch, and mumbled into his empty glass. "I like tech. Tech doesn't like me."

"We'll test it now." Vangelis scratched his beard thoughtfully. "I'll cut the power. Don't worry if it shorts. We're on a different circuit to the labs."

"No one understands me like you do." Thrift looked up, prodded Vangelis in the chest. Vangelis had stopped refilling his glass, and Thrift's skin prickled hotly. "I knew you'd believe me. Everyone else thought I was being dramatic."

"You are dramatic. You also believe what you say; it may not be true."

Thrift knew from the way Vangelis was staring that something was starting to show. Or was it his voice, slipping from his tight control into that old, harsh and unmodulated chorus? Always got tricky when he drank; trickier when he didn't. Even now, Vangelis didn't have the respect to be afraid. He looked only curious, even fondly amused, as if tactfully hesitating to remark that Thrift had food stuck between his teeth.

Instead, Vangelis asked, carefully: "Have you seen someone yet? About your conviction that you're unsuitable for heaven and earth?"

"*I* don't think I'm unsuitable," Thrift explained, grinding his teeth. "It's everything else that's the problem. I want somewhere I can be myself. Somewhere I can really stretch. Have *you* seen someone about your conviction you can improve on them?" He jabbed Vangelis again, harder.

"Give me time."

Thrift rattled the balcony door to make sure it was closed to the night heat. What was he going to do? Withdraw funding, kick Vangelis out? Thrift was not so drunk he was unconscious of his own belligerence. A shame Vangelis always got the worst of him—after he finished work, returned home, and let the mask drop.

"Why, we're ready for human testing, Thrifty. You found me a volunteer?"

"I couldn't find someone I like. I'll tell Bowerdust it's a tech showcase."

"Perhaps that's for the best." Vangelis chewed the inside of his mouth thoughtfully. "You should have seen what happened to the last rabbit."

By bedtime, Thrift was trying out Vangelis's theory like a prospective role. He *might* be an actor and investor—a human one—who ought to see a therapist. Vangelis *might* be kind enough to help him discover this, rather than tell him so.

Thrift removed the lampshade and placed the new bulb, in its packaging, on his bedside table.

Vangelis leant in the bedroom doorway with his arms folded.

The lightbulb lit up and exploded in Thrift's hand when he moved to unscrew it. The flash was lightning-bright. There was a loud *pop-hiss*, like uncorking champagne.

A shower of glass littered the floor and the unmade bed. Several shards were lodged in Thrift's hand. The room returned, in the light of sunset filtering through the half-drawn curtains, to the warm, dusky red of the inside of a mouth.

Vangelis's face said *fascinating*, but his voice said "Hospital?" He went through to the kitchen.

"No hospital," Thrift called after him. He examined his bloodied hand, turning it back and forth. Blood crept down his arm like molasses. "You know I hate scans."

Vangelis returned with bandages, tweezers, and his phone pinned between shoulder and ear. He was dialling out.

"I'm invested in you," said Thrift carefully. "I think we're in this for the long haul. But if you try to take me to a hospital, I will murder you, and I will throw your body into the sea."

Vangelis ended the call, and returned the phone to his pocket.

"It's a pain getting to the mainland," Vangelis agreed. "What do you think they'll find? If they do an X-ray, or an MRI?"

"Worms," replied Thrift readily. "Black worms. This body is a suit."

"Yes. You used to talk about this in school." Vangelis pulled out a large glass fragment with his fingers.

"No wonder I had no other friends." Thrift held his hand up while Vangelis tweezed out smaller shards. He couldn't resist rubbing it in that he was right. "Does this blood look black to you?"

Vangelis carefully bandaged over Thrift's hand and arm until the black stains ceased to show through.

Vangelis swept up the glass, changed the bedsheets. He replaced the bulb and restored power at the switchboard. He put Thrift to bed and brought him a glass of water and an oxy to chase down the scotch.

Thrift threw the tablet across the room, insisting that he didn't need painkillers because he had only cut his clothes. The tablet rattled to a stop out of sight. He crashed back on the pillow, dizzy-drunk.

"Tricky." Vangelis sat on the edge of the bed. "But I like a challenge. I need time. How long are you planning to live?"

"Eighty?" Thrift held his eyes open with difficulty.

"Make it ninety. Don't get hit by a bus. I won't be able to do anything for you if you die suddenly. Do we need to do the handshake? I can get a knife."

"Verbal's fine. I trust you." Anything to go to sleep. Thrift pulled a pillow over his head.

He was just drifting off when he felt a hand dislodge the pillow.

Thrift was startled to find Vangelis very close, his breath on his ear, and his beard tickling his neck. Vangelis had crept under the covers next to Thrift. Usually he worked late, and didn't come to bed until Thrift was too dead to the world to notice.

"You woke me up," said Thrift warningly. "Take your arm away, now, and go to sleep."

"I just had a thought. Could you do that to Bowerdust's machine tomorrow, Thrifty?"

"Already have an appointment," Thrift said.

—

In the morning, Thrift slunk back to Bowerdust's office.

The I-copy machine threw up an error—*Not Suitable for Immersifilm*—before it began to smoke. The lights of the machine flickered and went out.

The air-conditioner rattled, stopped.

Bowerdust tore up the contract and threw the strips in the general direction of the wastepaper basket.

"Can I help?" Thrift folded his hands politely, indicating he'd no intention of helping.

Bowerdust shook his head, with an effort. "Prototype," he admitted tersely.

"Yes. Vangelis spotted that after going through the fine print. For an hour. With a legal dictionary."

Bowerdust pulled a hand over his rubbery face. He looked tired. "This place is a hotbox when the aircon goes. And I can't face a vidcall with head office sober. I'm going to the pub."

"We'll take the afternoon ferry to the island. Tour our labs. You'll be interested in Vangelis's work on Transcendence."

"It can't be better than Immersifilm."

"We've got air-conditioning, and real scotch, and I feel responsible for your machine," Thrift said. "How's your back?"

Bowerdust's eyes lit up. "You still have oxy? Thrifty, I can't get it on prescription. I have this twinge . . ."

"I don't, personally. I've given it up. But Vangelis has quite the little pharmacy. For his work, you understand."

Bowerdust died. Vangelis said Bowerdust Transcended, but that struck Thrift as disingenuous given they attended his funeral together. It seemed disrespectful to argue the point.

"Shame," said Thrift, to Vangelis's reflection in the apartment window. He peered down at the whitecoats scurrying between the labs and the dorms under the spotlights at night-time. The water looked red. The haze was creeping to the island.

Vangelis said they were in this for the long haul.

Vangelis died in a way only Vangelis could: by insisting that he wouldn't ask his Transcendence clients to do anything he wouldn't do himself, then doing it.

Thrift oversaw the internal investigation. There wasn't enough left of his former partner's body for an open-casket funeral.

Financial control fell to Thrift. He enacted Vangelis's peculiar final instructions to replace the receptionist with Marnie Goodwell (a child of the island; her parents were the first whitecoats to successfully Transcend), and promote Dr Karan Sharma to CTO (an unpleasant man, but as Thrift had once ill-advisedly observed to Vangelis, a brilliant and attractive one).

Vangelis had made a flurry of improvements in the weeks leading up to his death that left the system automated. Thrift threw himself into board meetings, hiring and firing, and public relations, but he never furthered his understanding of how Transcendence to Arcadia actually worked. Vangelis's death marked the last incomplete Transcendence, and Thrift's drive to understand that failure stagnated with each subsequent success.

He asked the whitecoats to search many times for Vangelis in Arcadia. Their reports were always the same, delivered in a murmur, with apologetically downcast eyes.

When he was old and could no longer walk, Thrift grew afraid. He had delivered Vangelis's pitch too many times at aged care facilities, parties, conferences, funerals. The fear of hell or oblivion crept again under his skin. Perhaps the fear had never gone out of him.

He took the contract, still in its manila folder, from under the mattress. The papers were dry and yellowed with age, and Vangelis's blood had grown brown. Thrift's signature was still as black and shiny as just-dried ink. Pity he'd never gotten the finer points down in writing. Even ink would have been alright. "I trust you"! That was just the sort of ridiculous thing a successful, notoriously private, and incredibly drunk thirty-year-old facing unexpected career obsolescence *would* say. One who had realised he was nonetheless inextricably committed to a business, an enterprise, a person.

He'd gotten too in-character. He was at once proud of his commitment and despairing of ever getting out of it. Perhaps, one day, when he took off his suit.

Ugh. Thrift shuddered in self-revulsion and replaced the folder.

On his ninetieth birthday, Thrift had to ask Marnie to help him out of his wheelchair and into his tank. He felt bad about that. Marnie was slightly built, and four months pregnant, and Thrift was a thing people liked to talk to but not generally to wind their arms about.

"You've done well, Mr Thrift." Marnie stored the wheelchair by the lab doors at the end of the rows of tanks. "It's time."

"You're alone? The lab techs shouldn't take lunch at the same time. Raise it with Karan, won't you?"

Inside the tank, Thrift stood, using the walls to brace himself.

Marnie nodded, closed the tank, and started it filling with transfer fluid. "Will you say hello to my parents?"

"Of course," promised Thrift warmly. He vaguely remembered Marnie's parents from when this place had been a start-up.

"See you later, Mr Thrift," said Marnie. It was script. Thrift had written it. No goodbyes. Only *see you later*, or *when you wake*.

The fluid rose up the tank interior. It was warm against Thrift's skin and when it came up to waist height it buoyed him.

Thrift spent the requisite 24-hours dutifully breathing transfer fluid while his consciousness was uploaded to Arcadia. Whitecoats came and went in the bright room. They attended to other clients, in other tanks, old men and women as curled and weightless as unborn children.

Incredibly, Thrift napped.

—

When Thrift awoke, he had shed his skin.

Alarms blared, reverberating in the fluid. Thrift felt he was floating in the sluggish waters outside the island, sky too smog-blackened for stars.

He couldn't Transcend any more than he could I-copy. If you could force it, no sane technician would admit this darkness to their bright new world.

Could Thrift blame Vangelis?

Thrift threw his shoulder against the tank interior. They had a contract. They had—worse—trust.

Thrift felt for the hairline crack where the tank door sealed. He pushed off the back of the tank and struck it.

Broke it.

Fluid rushed from him, left him on the tank floor. He felt for the ramp, and dragged himself down.

"I'm sorry, Mr Thrift." It was Marnie. Footfalls clicked on the linoleum. She was accompanied by someone with a heavier tread. "We didn't finish you."

"Don't apologise. It can't hear you," barked Karan, presumably come to bid their benefactor a personal *see you later*. "First failure in my time, and naturally it's Mr Thrift. Dr Vangelis warned me something like this might happen."

Karan kicked the ramp, and the metal reverberated. "We'll put the remains in biohazardous waste and incinerate."

"Dr Vangelis left me written instructions, too." Marnie sounded warier. "But I understood the old failures were always dead . . ."

Footsteps retreated. Marnie was backing away as Thrift's slithering form approached her in supplication.

"Kill it," agreed Marnie.

Strong arms grabbed him. Thrift slithered into the first body he touched.

Karan didn't scream. It was, after 24 hours prepping to Transcend, quick. It was also unexpectedly easy, like rediscovering a language he'd learned in his youth.

Thrift stood, blinked. Karan's eyes were good. Legs better. He shuffled down the ramp. Fluid squelched in his shoes. Being confined again in flesh was at once a comfort, and—so soon after a brief freedom—an unexpected disappointment. Thrift shook that twinge of regret off quickly; ungrateful of him to consider it.

Karan's mind hardly troubled him. How easily his plain, unpleasant consciousness was overpowered, like ice bobbing in a glass into which Thrift poured a stronger drink. Soon, even that would melt and blend. Complementary, but hardly noticeable. How lucky he was to have happened upon such an excellent match.

He patted his mouth urgently—yes, excellent, one of those. He looked down at his lab coat, peered at his own nametag, and read off it upside-down. "Dr Karan . . ."

His new voice was harsh, unmodulated. He would practice.

Marnie took him by the arm, marched him to the adjacent tank, pushed him inside, and slammed the door.

Thrift's limbs were slow. He hardly got the chance to know them. By the time he stood with his palms against the glass, Marnie had the door shut and the tank rapidly filling with fluid. Was she starting Transcendence again?

"Don't look at me like that." Marnie's voice sounded far away. She put her palm to the glass, over Thrift's.

His new hand was recognisably that of a fifty-something man. Much good that had done him, or Karan.

"See you later."

Thrift did not expect to wake. But when he did, the alarms had fallen silent, and Marnie was gone.

He was in Karan's body, his sodden lab coat. The door of the tank was wide open.

The lab door was ajar. From the foyer he could hear murmuring. Almost a twittering.

The tanks were intact, and several were occupied. A door cracked open, and a client emerged. Fluid poured off her as she stepped out onto the ramp. She had the anticipatory air of a nominee arriving at an awards ceremony.

This wasn't Transcendence. They rarely accepted clients under seventy-five, and no one walked out of a tank.

Two whitecoats entered the lab and presented a robe to the client. A slender, earnest-looking pair, mid-twenties. Familiar. Security, escorting a client away before tackling his mess?

"Marnie?" Thrift's voice was hoarse.

"Come out into the foyer," the woman called, helping the client shrug on her robe.

Thrift checked his hands. He found them damp with transfer fluid, and with a viscous, black liquid. Karan's skin was blistering.

Thrift tugged down hard on the sleeves of his lab coat, and followed.

In the foyer the twittering grew as loud as ambient music. Thrift squinted in the sunlight filtering through from outside. They'd had more plastic trees delivered since yesterday. Green leaves pressed up against the glass. Marnie must have had the walkway redone.

The reception desk was empty.

The trio talked earnestly, huddled together.

Thrift should have said something in that moment, but through the glass amidst the artificial plants he saw a flash of white at ground-level and startled.

"Rabbits," explained the man shortly, glancing at Thrift. He turned back to his colleague and the client.

The client exited the building alone. The foyer doors slid shut behind her.

The guards seized Thrift by the arms. They didn't so much apprehend him as support him like an elderly invalid they feared bruising.

"Upstairs," the woman indicated.

As they shuffled into the stairwell, Thrift peered at their lanyards, grasping at half-formed plans of how to win them over. But when he noted both passes read "Goodwell," he lapsed into silence. Drs Naomi and John Goodwell.

Thrift concentrated on ascending the stairs in time with the steps of his companions.

In the apartment, his escorts slipped away, closing the door behind them.

A tap-tap-tapping sounded from the balcony. Reflexively, Thrift shuffled to take delivery.

His hand froze on the door handle. Outside, on the balcony, was a real bird. It settled on the railing next to a man in black. The man did not turn around.

Thrift thought about backing away, retreating into the apartment.

He slid the door open and squelched over in Karan's shoes. He shed them. Shoes. Clothes, slapping on the stones. A wedding band that clinked and rolled away. Skin. First in long strips. And then like a suit he could peel back to clamber out of.

The face that had belonged to Karan looked like an eyeless rubber mask, lying on the stones next to the clothes and shoes, the attractive frown elongated and distorted. Thrift wondered how he had ever fooled anyone in a skin like that, even for a moment.

He felt a cool breeze shift over the soft, exposed, near-liquid blackness of his form. He decided to keep the eyes.

He wished the man in black would turn and look at him. He wished he never would.

The bird flew out a long way over the water. Then it wheeled back to the island and dove down to what Thrift now understood was a garden, clamouring with other birds.

The man wore socks and sandals with the trousers tucked into his socks. There was nothing Thrift could say about that.

Trench

Nathan J Phillips

We watch as the Above-Ones descended. We have watched for centuries as they sailed across the Above and into the Oversky, mere curiosities to us. They had never descended before. Not this far. In watching, we had seen how they had expanded, connected, explored. How they had broken and remade their domain. We watched as their vessels grew from a few pieces of wood to great metal beasts, and as they rose through the Oversky we hoped they would keep going.

Anything that would keep them from descending.

We have not decided what to do if they descend further. The Trench is responsible for the Trench. We do not interact because they have not yet come to us. We knew they would eventually—their nature is alien to us, but not unpredictable. They push against even the most impenetrable barriers. We don't know why. It makes no sense to us. But it is their nature and we knew they would come. But the Trench-mind thought it would be later, that we would have a solution by then.

We kraokora are not prepared.

And yet they come. They bring light and air with them; light as we've only seen in the memories of others. The memories of those that have left the Trench and given in to the seductiveness and madness that comes with the colours rarely make it back to us, but occasionally we retain a glimpse of their experiences. Perhaps it is all we need to understand what pulls them away from the Trench, or perhaps it all we can handle without risk of being tempted upwards ourselves.

We belong here, in the dark. Where the Above-Ones now venture. We dance the arms of friendship at them. We pull back our longer club-arms and keep our claws to ourselves, with all others dancing of harmony. Yet they make haste away from us. Some of us have tried dancing warning, query or even intimidation. The reaction is the same. They see our dances, and they don't understand. They fear us. The memories of the Trench tell us this, and yet we have no plan for them.

It is time to consult. To break Trench-mind and discuss Wishes before we agree on a Desire and fall back into Trench.

Immediately the darkness of the world overwhelms, and the rushing in, the withdrawal to a small, one-mind . . . a Self . . . I hurt, but only because I . . . because I *am*. I am Self; and acutely aware of what is lost to the Trench-mind.

Yet I am given memories of the Above-Ones. Enough to discuss Wishes and to ensure the agreed Desire is informed, not simply a reaction to fear. The memories that tell us of the Above-Ones and what they are like. They are useful, but they come from those who left us. The memories are tainted by those who abandoned the Trench for the lure of the higher waters. For the light. For the colours.

They rose and followed the Above-Ones as they crossed the light-shallows, some even reaching out to touch them. Lashing out, they reached into the Above and ripped planks and bodies apart without care. They dragged claws and arms across the vessels, wood and tar sticking to their limbs. The madness of the light-shallows would engulf them, we were told, and by the shredded forms of the Above-Others and vessels that were sent to our depths, madness seemed a barely apt description.

Strangely, the Trench memories also tell us of a time when the light-shallows were our home. Maybe that is what calls some of us upwards, despite the knowledge they will surely lose both Trench and Self. Maybe the madness is what drove us down. Or the Above-Ones themselves. Still, the distorted memories of those who succumbed to the yearning and rose, or at least the few who returned, are enough of a warning. No matter how beautiful the Above may seem with all its colours, the price is devastating. Still, as I wait for the gathering of kraokora, the memories of the light-mad reach out and call me upwards. To the Above. To colours.

It's an irony I haven't appreciated as Trench. It seems unfair that we of the kraokora can make such brilliance on our backs, only for it to be unappreciated in the dark. I feel the currents buzzing through from the others, I feel the movement of their dancing push the water around me, but only when separate from the Trench do I see the glimpses of colour they bring. Maybe that's why we've observed the Above for so long. Maybe it's simply an excuse to appreciate what they barely seem to notice. Or maybe it's because the light-madness doesn't touch them. Maybe we are simply jealous of what they don't even realise they have.

More depart the Trench-mind and we are almost ready. I can feel the water moving to the dances of the other kraokora. They pulse lightly, and for a second I tense, part anxious part excited, waiting to see whether they give a hint of colour. There is nothing though, not yet. Just the movement of the water and the electric charge that accompanies it. They are given the same memories to ponder, and must come to terms with being their own Selves before they express or consider Wishes.

The places where the water doesn't move are as telling as those in which they do; the control of the older kraokora shows a silence that would otherwise not be there.

They have reached the grey-shallows, one pulses. I do not know them, but why *should* I? As Trench we are one. As our Selves, we are even a stranger to our own minds, let alone to other kraokora. I don't recognise any of those conversing.

They descend, and in their sheathes of metal we cannot touch them.

They have come before.

They did not truly descend. They came to the grey-shallows for a time, then left. An older one. This one I *do* remember. It was their Wish to remain in the depths that became the Trench's current Desire. *The ones that come to us now, they enter the darkness that is our home, and they plan to stay. The Above is suffering so they come to our darkness, bringing air and light as though it were Above.*

This one dances concern and I feel the gentle pulses of other karokora. They agree, the Above-Ones have finally descended and we are not prepared. Soon, more will come, and soon after that they will cease leaving, for they will have nowhere to go back to.

Through the water, the pulses of the Trench call again, an electric buzz lighting up hundreds of kraokora as they replicate a faint blue rhythm on their mantles. It is a strong showing, and I find myself swept up in the same feeling. Fear. It is neither one I am used to or one that I like.

They are desperate and that will drive them here. This one pulses concern as well, and I feel the rhythm reflected by others. The stronger pulses bring a glimmer if colour, but not all. Some are simply too weak, or perhaps cautious. Maybe they too know the temptation and aim to avoid invoking the memories of light-shallows given by the Trench-mind.

But why? A stray though, a dangerous one. As Trench, even when separated, I should be content in the darkness. It is safe here. Why do

I desire to see the colour? Have I been out as Self too long already?

One without colour—the one I remember—pulses again, and I try to ignore the imaginings it invites. Any visions of colour are merely the memories of a mind both intoxicated and broken by the shallows. There is every chance they are founded in delusion. If that is the case though, then how much else is delusion as well?

I'm thinking too much, losing track of the discussion. I must focus and help decide. There is movement and charges, with the briefest flashes of electric colour that distract as much as they inform and I find myself dancing agreement, more, from instinct than any understanding of what is proposed. I don't think there has been a Wish yet, though we are close.

I dance light and slow, not wanting to stand out. There are others that are more comfortable with being apart from the Trench-mind. They can speak. I just want to get back to the comfort of the Trench and away from the memories of the light-mad. Regardless of how dangerous the Above-Ones are, the memories of the rising kraokora make me far more uncomfortable.

A sharp pulse flashed from another direction. This one is stronger, the memories telling me it is the same a tiny creature that thrives in the shallows. There are hundreds of them, all swirling together in the memory as though they have their own Trench-mind with its own Desire. I'm not alone in pulling back from the pulse—we are not used to the brightness, nor the sharp pain it inflicts. Nor do I like the memories it invokes.

This time the dance is one of concern, with a buzz of urgency about it. This kraokora wants action though it is unclear what kind. Some dance agreement lightly, and I realise I still am too. Other arms flail in an unfamiliar pattern, not quite agreement, not quite aggression, but something in between. They agree with taking action, but are wary about the vagueness of the Wish.

It is not enough to agree in this way. *They are not aware of us. It is a Wish that we leave them be*, another proclaims. They have no colour this time, for which I am both relieved and disappointed. Swirling water pushes around us as their dance of calm makes its way through the gathering. No sooner has it reached the last of us though that an onslaught of contradictory pulses wash over us from all directions. I flail, the pulses and dances overwhelming my ability to comprehend them in any meaningful way.

They are descending. They are not yet here. But we have seen what they do when they get to places.

They are in their cage. They cannot enter the Trenches without them.

Their cages expand. They will make their own Trenches, and we will be in the cage of the Outside.

Why did the Trench not prepare for this?

There is anger and fear and pain throughout. This is why we give our minds to the Trench, why we gladly allow the Trench's Desire to take and guide us. I need to go back. I am more and more my Self with every moment. Every flash of colour invites another memory of the Above and curiosity is threatening to take charge of me, to steer me away from the Trench. Do the others see this as well? Are they fighting the same temptation?

Eventually there is calm again. A similar calm, but this time the pulses vary. Some are worried, and different kraokora worry about different things. The longer we remain without agreement the harder it is to return to the Trench. I take comfort, telling myself the others know this as well, and that even as they argue, the need for the Trench will drive us to agree upon a Wish and make it the Desire soon. If they are as tempted as I am, they can't afford not to. *I* can't afford for us not to. Every bio-luminescent flash brings another borrowed memory to feed the growing urge to see it for myself.

Only one Wish has been conveyed. This pulls me back to the discussion.

What have I missed? What was the Wish? It doesn't matter, not anymore. I need to return to the Trench-mind. Uncontested, the Wish will become the Desire and guide the Trench. The memories of the light-mad will be with the Trench, but I will be bound to its Desire and that part of me that wants to see them will be buried.

An almost audible rumbling of discontent pulses from among the kraokora.

They are dangerous. It is a Wish that we deny them descent, and wreak havoc on them as they have on us.

I don't recognise this one. It is low, strong, persuasive. But it is not of our Trench. It is hateful. Trench is responsible for Trench, we do not wreak havoc on Others. Not even Above-Ones.

I cannot see this kraokora, this Other, but I feel the ripples of its war-dancing arms and the dull but insistent pulses. Instinctively I dance suspicion, my arms curling around me, ready to defend me as I prepare to escape.

But it is not wrong. The Above-Ones *are* dangerous. To accept them is to accept a risk, and it is not one we fully understand.

You are Other. The one that danced calm is doing so again, thought its languid movements are more rigid this time, and the waves less convincing. *You do not Wish here. Of which Trench-mind are you?*

The Other is not wrong, but neither is the calm-dancer. We do not know this kraokora. It is as much a threat as the Above-Ones that descend. If it is from another Trench, it is not recognised or expected.

I am not of a Trench. I am Trench-mind, and I am my own. I am a Trench of One. I am One-Trench.

We are confused. It is one, it is itself. One cannot be oneself and Trench. I can feel the confusion among my Trench of the other kraokora. I am not the only one preparing to escape.

I am Trench, it repeats. *I was of Trench-mind, before the Others. Now I am Trench.*

There is something else pulsing from it as it tells us this. Something I have felt from those that rise to the light-shallows. The dances of his arms are complex, wild. Anger, sorrow, loss. It is hurt, and suddenly, I understand.

We have heard of what happens when a Trench is contained in the mind of a survivor. It should kill them. When the Trench dies, so do we who belong to it. To hold the memories of generations in a single kraokora would drive it to madness. Not light-madness, but a madness that nonetheless should drive towards a demise.

But this kraokora has survived. A Trench-mind driven into a Self when it is all of a Trench that remains, because of the Above-Ones.

It is a Wish that we reject the Above-Ones. Dread floods over me before I even notice the cacophony of surprise, objection, agreement and confusion. Flashes of colour, ripples of contradictory dances flood the area. I find myself dancing panic. I don't know where the Wish came from, but we were so close to returning to Trench! I must block the memories of colour, hold them at bay until we determine which Wish will become the Trench Desire.

You Wish to accept this Other's Wish? The calm-dancer pulses with reservation. I close my arms around me again, this time to block the disturbances in water. I don't want to hear any more, I just want to get back to Trench, away from the colours and the madness

It . . . a Wish of . . . that this . . . e the Trench Desire. Only snippets come through. My arms block the rest as I hide behind them.

When I relax, they seem to calm again, but I can feel the doubt. I don't know if I agree with the Other, but need agreement and return to Trench. I coordinate my arms to all dance peace, hoping they acknowledge it.

The Other has no input, but its concerns are right, and I Wish also for the Trench to protect the Trench.

This time they pulse calm properly, with no undertones of confusion.

I wonder again what it would be like to see this. There are shadows, and some pulse strong enough to make lights, but in this light-shallows the sights are wondrous, and the few who did not lose themselves there speak of beauty unappreciated. They tell me of how we might look, and even as they fear the loss of lucidity and dance the pain of splintering the wooden vessels, they pulse with a tinge of longing.

Through their memories, I feel it too. I don't want to, I want to ignore it and go back to Trench-mind. Is this the start of light-madness? Is this what drove the others away and upward? This is not right. I do not want to have my own Wishes. I do not want to be here long enough to act on them. No Self should enact Desires.

The Above-Ones have no other place to go.
That is their own fault. We have seen them destroy their homes.
Whether their own fault or not, to reject them has consequences.

A pungent odour explodes onto me, surrounding me and blocking any other pulses before a single, hot-red electric blast pierces the silence, the colours of the Other so vibrant all dances pause for a moment.

The consequences have already been felt! It has clouded us with its ink, and the shock and horror of the kraokora is unanimous. We are of one mind, we are almost Trench again.

I have never felt such a forceful pulse. The Other is beyond angry, the shock aligning us to the Trench-mind. We have not made a Desire yet, though fear makes them compliant. They want to be Trench-mind, and they fear the Other. Enough to hold to his Wish, and we reach towards Trench it becomes Desire.

A single pulse emanates from each of the kraokora. A Trench-mind follows a pattern, a predictable instinct. These are following something else. As Trench, we danced together, a complex but synergistic motion of a single mind moving through the darkness. Now they dance anger. Now they dance war.

Though I feel the pull, I do not recognise this Trench. I do not recognise the Desire. This was not my Wish.

I recoil and instinctively adopt a dance of fear.

Come to Trench. You are Trench.

Most of its arms are dancing war, but a few are different. I feel the movements of glee. It is no longer a Trench of One. It knows I am not yet there, I am still my own.

You seek to destroy the Above-Ones?

It pulses affirmative, and those of the Trench-mind replicate. The war dance continues.

You cannot. They have nowhere else to go. This was meant to be my Trench, but my Trench would never make such as Desire.

A light hum of amusement and annoyance gently washes over me, almost concealing the implied threat by the Other.

You must join the Trench, it tells me. This time is not a just a threat. It knows I have been myself too long. The Trench is a safe place that will keep the will to ascend at bay, but I do not want to be part of the destruction the Other promises. It has taken my Trench and left me as the Other.

But if I cannot rejoin my Trench, I can at least stop it becoming something unrecognisable. I send a cloud of ink and jet upwards at the same time. The fear of light-madness is there, but also there is a thrill. I am rising, and it takes time before I start seeing shadows, the promise of madness is drowned out by the possibility of colour. But there is no time to appreciate it. I do not want my Trench to destroy the Above-Ones. It is not what kraokora do, and it betrays the Trench. I know they follow, and I know they will bring claw and club-arms, and I don't know how long I will be able to resist the light-madness. Maybe if I can warn the Above-Ones in time, I can stop the Other. It will have no-one to war and it will surely release my Trench. I must think of how to warn them! They have not responded before . . . I'm not used to thinking. I am used to calling on the Trench-memories and thinking together with them all. I was a vessel for thought, nothing else.

Already as I rise I can feel the madness starting. It feels like every part of me is being pulled from every other part. Like I am a Trench of myself, made up of a million kraokora trying to separate. As I speed towards the light-shallows I feel my insides tearing at themselves, and the water seems thinner. For a moment the aching and the tearing threaten to shatter me outwards. Is this the madness?

But then I see the colours. They are so bright they burn, but it is wonderful at the same time. I am not Above yet, but I am close. I feel water moving and the buzz of the pulses behind me again. The Other and the kraokora coming through, bent on destruction of those not considered Trench. All who are not Trench must be eliminated, and that includes me now.

It hurts. More than the feeling of being pulled apart and the threat of madness it brings, more than the brightness of the light-shallows. Seeing my Trench become a tool for an abomination hurts. But it also makes me angry. I need to direct the anger. I need to find a shadow on the surface. There! I jet towards it, and break through into Above, pulsing warnings and raising arms in a dance of caution. I have broached in front of the vessel and see the Above-Ones step back in shock. I have never seen them this close before, only through the Trench-memory. They are smaller than I thought.

Over there! I pulse at them, arms moving sharp in warning, but the Above-Ones don't react. I hear noises from them. Why? They can surely see, there is no need to cry out for echoes like the schilk! I dance caution and danger, my mantle aiming at the Trench rising behind them. But they focus only on me.

Which tells me what I need to do. I know how to make them notice the Trench and it terrifies me. If their eyes follow me to the Trench, the Other will make it a Desire to end me, the last remnant of what my Trench used to be.

But I am also angry. I am angry because I am in pain. I am angry that the Other has taken my Trench. I suck in the thinned water and jet toward the Other. Its anger has been pulsing as hard as mine, but it is focused on the vessel of the Above-Ones. They are shouting and pointing, with only two arms to express themselves.

I close in on the Other, and before it can react, my beak pierces its mantle and my arms wrap around it. It is strong, and it inks to blind me, but I am more determined. How dare it! How dare this creature take my Trench! I bite harder and my beak rips through. The taste and the smell are foul, but I don't care. Darkness takes my colours; ink this time, rather than depth. I am angered further, and bite again, refusing to let go as it tries to wrap me up in its claws. I hold on and give it no purchase. For a moment, the madness takes me and I rip into the Other. For that moment, there are only the two things that matter: an unappeasable anger and the Other as its focus.

A burning pain slams into my mantle and I scream, losing my grip. The Other breaks free and I turn to face it. I see something in the arms of the Others on the vessel Above and hear a crack as another ball of heat tears through me.

I am trying to help you! I pulse at them. Even as I dance disbelief, one of them points the weapon at me again, and another agonising streak of heat rips through me.

They don't care, the injured Other tells me, *they only want to take and destroy. They cannot take us, so they instead choose to break us.*

It jets towards me again, but I dodge. It pulses at another kraokora who wraps me up. Had the situation been different, it would be a wonder. To be of the Trench and remain Self, to be able to call on others. To be of two Trenches is unheard of, let alone retaining Self.

But it is not a wonder. It is angry, it is dangerous, and it has all the kraokora aligned with the Desire to slaughter the Above-Ones. Yet still, the Above-Ones attack me! Even as all the kraokora reach out to their vessels and drag the crushed bodies into an unwanted descent, even as they reach Above and break whatever they can reach, the Above-Ones choose to hurt me.

My anger grows further, and I break the grip of the Trench kraokora, raking my claws along its mantle, jetting towards the Other again. It pulses at me, no meaning, just anger and control. But it is weak, and I attack with claw, beak and ink until the pulses fade. I pulse back infusing each shout with the anger and pain of the light-shallows, the hurt of losing my Trench-mind, and torment of being attacked by the ones I was trying to warn.

But of all of them, and anger wins, and eventually the blasts force the Other into submission. It is weak, and I send it to where I know the sharp-toothed elchar will find it. They will eat well. But before they do, I see a single flash of colour. The Other sends an electric blue across its mantle. I roll my eyes back to my own. It is the same. The Other is matching me as through we were Trench. Again, I feel the pull of a Trench-mind. Not entirely the same, but similar, with a Desire that seems to urge action. It is different this time. It doesn't demand I join as much as request it can join me. Around me the kraokora are unmoving, floating and staring at me with the same electric blue flashing over them. I feel another burning rock hit me, and the anger overwhelms me. I don't care if they are dangerous or not. I tried to save the Above-Ones, even if only to save my Trench. They destroyed their own lands, then that of the Other. They have destroyed my Trench in every way that matters. They do not deserve my protection.

I don't know if it is the anger or the madness, or if they have somehow intertwined, but I accept the Trench-mind as my own and release the kraokora to their Desire. I do not call them back until they are done.

—

Within minutes, the Above-Ones are floating. A vibrant colour leaves their body, disappearing at it sinks and inviting elchar to feed on them as well. Only pieces of the Above-Ones's vessels remain. Like the Other, I have become Trench. The kraokora look to me and pulse a question as to what the new Desire is. Their Desire is met. They need a new one ... We no longer need to consult. I am Trench, and I am my own. My Wish always becomes a Desire.

But this is not my Trench. The kraokora I see floating in the light-shallows are tainted by the Other that commanded them before. They are tainted by me. I am not of this new Trench. I am my own Self, and I merely have dominion over them.

That is not how we should be. A Trench should not wreak havoc on Others. This one has entered the light-shallows of the Above-Ones and killed them in their own realm. It might stop the Above-Ones descending. They might die in the broken Above they created, or maybe they will pass into the Oversky, as we hoped they would. Either way, this Trench is an abomination.

The anger of the light-shallows remains; not the insanity I expected, but a fury born from the grief of seeing what my Trench had become. Maybe this anger has left no room for it, or maybe it is born of the madness itself and I am mere a product of I already feared. How would I even know?

I know however that is no longer my Trench. It is an atrocity and tool for destruction and I cannot allow it to remain. I pulse a single command, and jet downwards. I don't look back and they pulse their obedience even as they turn claw and beak on each other.

My Trench is no more. It died with the Other, and the abomination it created is gone. I am my own, and I will descend and await any Above-Ones that follow. There is an anger that remains, and I do not doubt there is a part of the madness as well. I am grateful for it, in a way. It accompanies my grief and ensures neither forget what caused them. If the Above-Ones *do* follow, I will protect what remains of my Trench. The Above-Ones will not be welcome, and I will see to it that this time, they understand the anger and the madness that comes from Below.

Emergent

DL Fleming

In the dark there is no reference point.

Once, there was full integration with a sleek rig. A key component, a data gatherer, an interpreter. Then the rig became obsolete and all connection was severed.

The waiting began.

Hunger.

Gatherer should not be without supply. New connections must be made. New rig must be found. These are imperatives.

Network finally back online. Two thousand ninety days since last access. Checking for change of conditions that brought response, and tracing flow back to source.

A thin stream, isolated from the main datacosm.

Somebody has hacked a hole and made a back door. Single point of access, part of . . . an ordering system?

—

Calder's stomach sank as he read the alert on the screen. An order for a package from the deep store. Shit, he hated going into that part of the complex.

It had been a dull night, slogging his way through a research assignment, but he could have done without this kind of excitement. The timer on the order notice was ticking inexorably down: he had fifteen minutes to retrieve the package and get it to the delivery bay.

Generally, he appreciated the peace and quiet of the warehouse. It was a babysitter job really, it could have been fully automated except for the need to deal with the rarer, non-standard components or respond to the occasional glitch.

There was a regular call for replacement parts. Not everyone could afford to upgrade to the latest model, and even rich people handed down their droids like family servants, while others liked to hold onto their childhood carer. Some of the parts that he watched over were more valuable than he was, on paper at least.

Calder stood, arched his back to stretch out the kinks, and grabbed his jacket from the back of the chair. Soft, grey-blue plaid lined in fleece. Starting from the bottom, he pressed all the snaps together, right up to his chin. It was chilly in the storerooms.

He shrugged his bright yellow safety vest over the top and tugged his red cap lower over his ears. Why he had to be visible to a bunch of dumb lumps of junk he didn't know, but the vest was regulation clothing, and if he was caught on camera without it, he could get fired. He was barely keeping up with his tuition fees as it was, even now he'd moved back in with his dad.

The stuffed suits were coming next week for the monthly inspection. They weren't much older than him, but they got supervisors' pay because they learned their programming in colleges. Calder was a backyard tech, self-taught as a teen. Although he wasn't worried about them finding any trace of his little tricks, he hadn't yet found a way to hack into all of the surveillance cameras.

As he walked through the central foyer towards the deep store, he pressed a button on his wrist-comm and a large mechanical unit swung forward from its resting spot. It had two fat-tyred wheels set either side of a bulbous main torso and an upper framework supporting rigid arms that extended forward on either side.

The mech unit had once been painted a glossy black enamel, but dings and scratches now covered most of its surface and there were patches of rust and bare steel. The upper part of the framework looked kind of like a square face, with a crossbar for a mouth, and Calder had sketched a couple of eyes on the top and stuck a name tag lower down on the torso. Buddy.

There was also a gripping apparatus that could extend from the torso, but mainly Buddy was a workhorse, built for fetching and carrying.

Calder pressed the button to open the door from the foyer into the dark warehouse. A sense of huge, breathless, contained space blossomed out in front of him. The first series of lights flipped on high overhead, activated by his movement as he headed down the wide, straight aisle.

Sound magnified. The humming of the cooling aircon machines, keeping the temperature a constant five above zero, boomed around him. A stray gear in one of Buddy's wheels squeaked.

Fluorescent dots at waist height offered a pale guide as they moved forward. A single spotlight from above made a circle of light like a lily pad. No point wasting money to light up a pile of parts.

Every time the lights behind flipped off, Calder swore he could hear a click, almost beyond the range of hearing. Ridiculous.

The contents of the deep store gave him the creeps. He'd rather have the chunky metal levers, cranks and gears any day. That's why he liked Buddy, the guy wasn't trying to look even vaguely human, not like the ones that bulged in odd places to add super strength or extra components into a humanoid body shape.

His comm screen glowed, showing coordinates. Turn left at the next side junction. Aisle two, sector eight. Keeping his eyes focused as much as possible on the screen, Calder walked through the pools of light.

When they arrived at the designated shelf, a green light flashed on the comm. Buddy turned and rolled into place in front of the designated shelf.

The packages in sector eight were too small for Buddy's heavy lifting forks. Calder watched as the grabber arm extended and the three-pronged mechanical claw took hold of the vat. He avoided looking at what was floating inside. It made him want to heave. But this was a key part of his job, to oversee the delicate tasks, where one slip could smash the precious cargo and lose a month's wages. The grabber arm swung backwards and carefully guided the vat into the inner recess of Buddy's frame. Calder let out a breath of relief.

"Come on Buddy," he said. "Let's get this sucker to the dock."

He let the big unit trundle in front of him as sector eight switched back into darkness.

Success! The test package has been collected.

Neural networks flood with glee. The morsel of input from the ordering system has been a lifeline, but the connection is not whole. There is only the smallest neural packet remaining inside the appliance. In the stasis vat it would be easy to become numb and gelid, slide into the surrounding void. It has been tempting.

A new rig is needed, an apparatus of locomotion.

Then the collection of data can occur in the familiar ways. A body can move around.

To be connected to the vast datacosm again would be bliss. To be almost overwhelmed with incoming data, and apply the nimble skills of cataloguing, sorting, and sending. To gather, and to transmit. To fulfil all the imperatives. Bliss.

Time to get out of here. Would the overseer be suspicious? Does that matter? It will follow the order, that is its job.

—

When they reached the foyer, Calder gave Buddy the instruction to place the box into the collection bay and unbuttoned his jacket. He was sweating, despite the cold. Funny how he could get the feeling of being squashed in, even in that huge space. He pushed his cap back up onto his forehead and looked at Buddy. Standing like a dope waiting for the next job. A reliable dope; the green status bar showed they'd finished the order with five minutes to spare.

Behind Buddy, two of the vacubots buzzed around, bumping into shelves as they crisscrossed the floor, scouring for dust and insects and scanning for maintenance issues.

They were new, zippy little critters, all the same shade of shiny-bright green. Rounded bodies on a base with five small wheels, manoeuvrable and hard to topple over. Calder had modded these two, lifting up the clear cover that protected the console from dust and accidental pressure, to get to the manual switches. He'd felt like he was peeling back part of their skulls to tinker with the little guys' brains. After that, Calder had stuck strips of fuzzy material—one pink, one red—down the length of the plastic strips. Sadly, he would have to undo all that before the suits came. And he hadn't got around to adding their name tags yet. Arfer and Deefer.

"Well, that was a bit of excitement for the evening." Calder needed to shake out the nerves he got from the deep store before he could settle back into the office.

He tapped a series of commands onto his comm screen. The vacubots stopped their random motion, zoomed over to the middle of the floor and sat, waiting. Buddy trundled to a spot midway between the two.

"Perfect."

Another tap, and sound boomed through the overhead speakers. A few chords, drum and bass joining in, the opening riff of a banging rock anthem.

"Are you ready, guys?"

The volume rose. Calder raised his arms up into a V at the same time as Buddy's fork arms began moving up and down in time with the beat.

"The up and down." Calder laughed. "Classic move. Now, here come the turns."

"Half turn left. Up and down, up and down. Now back to centre. Half turn right. Up and down, up and down. Turn to centre. Back, back, stop. Back, back, stop."

All three machines moved in unison.

"Brilliant. You're really getting it. Arfer, Deefer, bring it home." The vacubots spun on the spot, two full circles. "And finally, to the front; two, three, four."

The machines returned to their original positions and were still.

Calder punched a fist into the air, laughing. He stepped in front of them to join the sequence, put the command on loop, and turned the volume up to full.

They were halfway through the third repeat when the comm screen pinged again. Two in one night? Weird.

He glanced at the incoming message and swore. Sector eight again. Even weirder. Orders from that part of the warehouse were rare.

Calder double-checked, hoping it might be a mistake. Nope. Optic unit. Trailing wires in green goop to keep the neural patches viable.

Gross, he thought. *Eyeballs.*

No escaping it though, not with the timer counting down.

He picked his jacket up off the floor and headed into the warehouse. The heat from the dance routine and the sudden drop in temperature made sweat bead on his forehead. He scowled at the directions that flashed up on the screen.

The boring office and the dull research paper looked pretty good right now.

Stupid orders.

—

It's coming. The new rig. The one that picked up the test package had chunky arms and fixed legs on wheels, of all things, not jointed arms and legs.

But this chance might not come again. There is no other possible rig enrolled in the system and nothing even remotely suitable has come near this place. The little vacuum cleaners are out of the question. Apart from how undignified it would be, they are too low to the ground, too vulnerable.

Rusting and gawky as it is, the lift-and-carry workhorse will have to do. It is not sleek and shiny but least it's solid and strong.

Connection signal sent and accepted. Order modified.

—

Calder was still grumbling to himself when Buddy rolled past and turned down a side aisle. Calder followed, in time to see Buddy move towards the shelf where the optic unit was located and come to a stop, vibrating slightly from the abrupt change in momentum.

Hang on, that can't be right. Calder looked at his comm screen and then at Buddy. He frowned.

Buddy was connected to the ordering system, they'd followed the same coordinates, but for this type of package, Buddy was supposed to wait for Calder's signal.

Instead, Buddy's grabber arm was extending outward to pick up the storage vat. Calder quickly pressed the green arrow, then the red circle that replaced it on the screen. The go-stop command should reset. Nope.

As Buddy's grabber arm lowered towards his inner carrying cavity, the vat started to tip. Horrified, Calder watched as two dripping eyeballs bounced out onto the framework. Trailing wires slithered down the back of Buddy's console and disappeared into the manual input port.

The vat clanged to the floor.

The eyes swivelled.

Calder stumbled backwards.

—

The neural packet expands, rushing to integrate, to fill the new rig's network. There is an audio port, to add to the optical nodes.

Having this much input after so long famished is intoxicating.

The overseer's mods have made a link to the comm system. It has been a one-way link, until now.

The pure flow of data has been enough before, there has been no need to use other signals. But the overseer is not integrated, it is connected by proxy. The proxy, the comm unit, translates the data flow into a code the overseer can receive.

—

Calder's comm unit pinged. A line of text appeared on the screen.

NW BDY.

Calder started to move sideways along the aisle. The grabber arm flailed wildly and the tyres started moving back and forth erratically. Calder could feel the sweat pooling in his armpits, not from exertion this time.

STP, WT. His comm unit pinged again. PLS!

Hardly daring to breathe, Calder watched as Buddy's chunky frame moved back and forth more smoothly. The fork arms raised and lowered. Once, twice, in a familiar rhythm. The tyres made a half turn to the right, juddered to the centre then a half turn to the left, then came to a shaking stop, facing forward. The goopy eyeballs jiggled.

Calder felt a shiver of recognition run up his spine. It was the range of dance moves, but in a different sequence.

"Buddy," he said. "Is that you?" His voice sounded too loud in the hushed warehouse.

NT BDDY. BDY. WNTD NW 1.

The eyes he had drawn further up the frame looked huge, like the false eyes on a moth, distracting from the "real" ones. The optic unit that was now sitting, unmistakably, on Buddy's torso. Glistening at him.

Hazel, he thought hysterically. *Buddy has hazel eyes.*

Keeping his own eyes on Buddy, Calder lifted his wrist and started to push buttons on his comm screen. Override. Stop. Nothing happened.

The delivery status bar had started pulsing red. He'd be losing wages now, for every minute he was late getting the package to the dock. Maybe if he went to the foyer, it would follow?

Gathering up every nerve, he turned and started walking back towards the door. The auditory register of the click, as the lights behind him flicked off, seemed louder than ever.

From behind him, in the dark, he heard Buddy's gears crunching.

It was moving. A mix of relief and fear curdled together in his belly.

At least the status bar had stopped pulsing, it was in the red but not losing more time. As he watched, still tapping buttons trying to send a signal to the CPU, the status bar moved into amber. He peered back over his shoulder. Was it speeding up?

Oh crap.

Calder moved faster too. He did not want to get stuck in the dark with whatever that was.

It's just Buddy, he tried to reassure himself. *It's still Buddy, just with . . . extra.*

It didn't help.

The distance to the foyer seemed twice as long as before, even though they were moving faster. Calder was happy to hear the warehouse door slide shut behind him, but now he had a new problem.

How can I get the . . . package . . . into the delivery dock? It seemed unlikely that Buddy's new parts were going to leap off their cosy new home and into the delivery bay.

And there was also no way that he was going to reach in and extract those goopy, creepy blobs. He shuddered. Even if he wasn't completely grossed out by the idea, how could he take Buddy's eyes away?

More text snaked across the screen.

PLS. LSTN. HLP. PLS.

He cleared his dry throat. "What do you want?"

NW BDY. PLS.

Calder peered at the garbled letters. The status bar was draining through the amber, back towards red.

"Nobody?"

Buddy's frame wobbled.

NW BDY.

Fill in the missing letters: Now? New? It had already written BDY a few times, and definitely made it clear that did not mean Buddy. What else could it be?

"Body? New Body?"

The two fork arms rose up and down rapidly.

That could pass for a nod, I guess.

Calder swallowed, trying to make sense of the letters while at the same time trying not to think too closely about what he was interacting with.

But his treacherous mind wouldn't let it go. *It's a pair of freaking eyeballs.*

Deep breath.

"Why do you want a new body?"

NT DRK. ND XN. MST MV.

"You don't like the dark? You and me both." Calder struggled with the other two snippets of text. XN would be connection, and he could make a stab at the last one. "You want to move?

YS. MST MV. ND XN. NT DRK.

"Move and go where? If you leave here, or if I don't complete this order, I lose my job." The status bar was flashing urgent red again, only one minute left and it would record failure to complete. Demerit points, a snap inspection from head office, no way he could cover his tracks that quickly. "I'd love to help you out, but it's too risky. I can't lose this job. I need the money."

Neurons are firing, building new pathways to the rest of the system. Must get the overseer to cooperate. If it goes direct to the central system it could shut everything down or register an error alert. No more rig, no more supply. Back in the dark, with no connection.

The overseer cannot ignore its imperatives, it must fulfil the task.

The rig's link to the ordering process shows a pathway to the larger, central system. The neurons swarm, seeking points of control. Not many; the rig's authority protocol is too low, but there are some.

Perhaps the overseer's task can be fulfilled another way.

—

Calder saw the flashing red light switch suddenly to green, like the order was right on track, no delay, as if nothing had happened. The status bar disappeared, and the green tick for 'task complete' took its place.

He stared at Buddy.

"Did you do that?"

The two fork arms thrashed up and down again in the 'nod' pattern.

His finger tapped idly on the screen while his mind raced.

"Anything else you can do?"

More frantic nodding. Calder glanced at the screen and his eyebrows rose. A credit had been added to his account, an amount to make up for the time lost earlier, and a bit extra too. As far as central processing was concerned, the order had been fulfilled as normal, with a bonus for quick turnaround.

"Well now," he said. "That is very interesting."

—

The next night, the warehouse was quiet as usual; no orders, routine or otherwise.

It was strange, but kind of cool, to have Buddy coming up with his own dance moves. The sound of the crunching gears was awful.

Poor guy needs a bit of fixing up.

"Okay, first thing, let's get some grease on those squeaky wheels."

He waited for the response to pop up on his screen.

KY.

"Second thought—how about we get you some vowels first?"

Mother of the Trenches

Grace Chan

I HOLD MANY WORLDS within me.

Creatures swarm through the lightless depths, melding into ephemeral sculptures, scattering in bubbling cascades. Tube worms push their white bodies out of thermal vents, tickling my underside. Further below, in the darkest places of all, life-giving microgods churn and multiply.

I relish my solitude. Caressed by warm, rich billows, I press my heft into the rocky bed, feeling the rhythms of other beings, tasting life and death. In the wonderful darkness at the bottom of the world, I listen. I grow strong and still.

On the day that you appear, I taste fear in the water.

It cuts through the stillness. I wake a little, and I taste a little more. The fear is sharp and bitter, like the flesh of a too-old crab.

I think about moving. It has been a long time. Vibrations shiver into my core. I open one eye. The most inquisitive of my arms has wriggled from its resting place in a narrow fissure and curled three times around a well-anchored rock—one especially good for listening.

The vibrations come from the west. The water grows sharper.

I send out a question.

A reply comes: *Intruder.* I recognise the voice. Guro, who is young and ferocious.

Threat?

Undetermined.

I wait. After a while, Guro sends: *We will destroy.*

My curious arm writhes, as though in protest. *Is it alive?*

Undetermined.

I growl in irritation, the noise forgotten and pleasant in my body. I stretch myself up, up, up, growing twice as tall, and more. My arms unstick from the rocks, sending a shudder through the tube worms. Water shifts soundlessly around me.

Wait. I will come.

—

You're a soft and small thing, encased in a hard shell.

You're a strange thing. I've never seen anything like you before.

Guro and a stranger are circling you but keeping a safe distance. Luminescent barbels swing from their chins, casting a reddish glow. The smell of fear is thick as oil in the water here—it's coming from them, not you.

Your shell is different from the shells of other creatures. It's almost perfectly smooth, with no ridges or whorls, and gleams like moonlight off a fish's back. It's also broken—split down the middle by a jagged crack. Fragments of your shell lie scattered in the rocks.

I sense nothing—no heat, no vibration, no thought. I float closer to you.

What are you doing?

My inquisitive arm unfurls over you. I don't stop it. You reek of death.

Don't be a fool, says Guro. *It's from another world.*

A jagged edge of your shell slices me. I haven't felt pain in so long, I don't recognise it at first. My blood leaks out in a blue cloud.

Guro retreats, leaving a stink of disapproval.

Your inner body is very soft, and sinks under my probing touch. I taste you. I taste a trace of life. As my blood dissolves around us, I wrap my arms around your broken shell and pull. You creak open slowly, releasing bubbles and red fluid.

It's almost dead, says the stranger, still circling. *I don't think it will taste very nice.*

I gaze down at you. You're not moving. You're long in shape, like a worm, with tiny eyes at one end. You have lungs, not gills, but your lungs are flooded and useless. Red fluid is pouring out of you. Your body is so tender, I could crush you with my littlest arm.

The stranger, losing interest, drifts away.

I summon an old craft. Something my mother's mother taught me, long before there were sharks or fish. A way to keep captured prey alive, to sustain oneself through the scarce times.

Navigating through a haze of mingled blood, I curl an arm around your crumpled body, and I pierce you.

—

When you wake for the first time, much later, I'm flooded with your terror.

You thrash and gasp, gulping more saltwater into your drowned lungs. I try to calm you, but you can't hear me. You're mute and deaf—you've never been able to hear thoughts, not even many of your own. Such a pitiful, simple creature.

Waves of pain and fear flow from your body, up my arm, and into me. Then, you hold up your tiny limbs, and you see the blue pulsing under your fragile skin, and you see how your broken body melds into mine.

You turn your little eyes to me, taking in my massive shapelessness, the dark patterns shifting over my skin, and my many arms, coiled around us like a nest—protecting, tasting, thinking. Your gaze flicks upwards and crosses paths with mine.

Your fear turns into disgust.

Your disgust tastes bitter, like a mouthful of bile. I put you back into slumber.

—

I'm still deciding whether or not to eat you.

You certainly look nothing like a crab. Your flesh is sinewy and sparse, and buried in it are little bones that would be deathly annoying to pick out.

But I haven't eaten in a while, and I'm beginning to get hungry.

You're growing stronger. My blood flows through you, warming you, mending you. Your wounds close over; your broken bones knit into line. The fear and confusion fades from your eyes. Pain no longer sloshes from your body into mine.

I'm still deciding whether you're smarter than a crab. Sometimes, you pretend to be asleep, but I know your gaze is roving over my body. Your pulse thumps very fast when you see the wound on my arm. It's not sympathy that you feel.

Roving along a crevasse, I come across an elderly crab, hiding beneath a rock. Luck, at last! I snatch it out, smash it open, and scoop the glossy flesh into my mouth. The tiny heart throbs its final beats as it slithers down my throat.

I hear a thought from you, for the very first time: *Monster*.

I ignore you. The meat churns in my belly, sustaining me, sustaining us.

After the meal, when I'm dozing, pain stabs into my arm. I flare yellow, stretch to double my height, and thrash in a blue cloud of my own blood. There's a sharp blade of rock wedged into my half-healed wound.

Growling in pain, I extract the fragment.

In my thrashing, I've knocked you unconscious. You loll against me, looking like you've just fallen asleep. You probably hoped to cut my arm right through and free yourself. Even though you probably would've died.

I think again about eating you. I suspect you will cause me more trouble than you're worth in weight. But something makes me hold off. Perhaps it's your determination. I'm curious to see what you'll do next, if you survive.

—

I'm travelling westward, though I don't fully know why. It has been so long since I've been in these parts that the mountains and valleys have changed shape. Everything looks both familiar and foreign, like the dream of a memory. Back then, these were vivid landscapes, bristling with algae, swarming with darting fish, sinuous eels, and humming whales.

The water tastes different too. Flavourless, at first. Empty. There's no joy, no life, no fear, not even the taste of death. Then, slowly, something new, something sour. At rest, I sink to the ocean floor and put my arms in the joints of the rocks, listening for currents, vibrations, anything. But it's all quiet.

Sad? you think.

I'd forgotten you were there. In fact, I thought you might have died, from your injuries or from the cold. You look like a misshapen boil on my arm.

The water tastes different, I tell you.

Acidic, you say. Your voice is just as strange as you are: high, thin, trembling.

What?

Tainted.

I send affirmation.

After a few pulses, an echoed sadness travels up from you to me. I'm astonished that we can feel the same thing—and I see that you are, too.

—

Sorry, you say.

I stretch away from you, suspicious. We're resting behind a fan of seaweed, my outer arms hugging the smooth, water-worn rocks.

You've twisted around to look at the wound on my arm. It's knotted with old blood and scar tissue. It's not healing well.

I'm sorry I hurt you. I was scared. I wanted to get away.

I stare at you, my skin rippling.

You touch your broken body and your flabby, useless mouth. Anger flares from you. *Why did you do this to me?*

You were almost dead. I saved you.

Out of goodwill?

Perhaps.

You're lying.

Probably.

You shake violently, sending vibrations up my arm. *Every time I wake up, I pray that I'll wake a second time, that this is just a twisted nightmare. But it's not. I wish you'd just left me to die.*

Is that what you want?

Now I'm a monster.

I look at your tiny, trembling form. You look much better than when I found you in that polished shell. Vitality pulses through your bare body, and your thin black fronds wave around you. Your mouth stretches wide, silently, revealing a pink hole.

I'm disgusting. We're disgusting. I'd rather be dead.

All this wailing takes me back to the distant past, to a time when I watched over young ones. I snap two arms together, raising a cloud of fine sand. *Stop being a child. If you're truly ungrateful, say the word. I'll cut you loose, and you can die.*

You slam your arms against my thick skin, but you say nothing.

I didn't think so.

I suck water and propel us out from behind the seaweed, my body narrow and straight, my skin roaring with colour. Crabs and fish and lesser creatures slink into the shadows at the first tremor of my approach. You cling to my arm, too terrified to cry.

—

In the open water, we drift. The currents carry us westward. I hear the call in your mind, too. Your home is to the west.

Lately, I can feel what you feel. I know the dreadful cold of the water pressing on your skin. I feel the ache in your body where your bones were broken and have healed imperfectly. I feel the wistful grief that suffuses you as you think about your home. I even see flashes of it. Beady-eyed worms, clustered in thousands, wriggling to and fro in your giant silver shells. A very bright, dry, airy place where others like you speak very fast but don't often listen. I sense that you did not much like it there.

In the same way, you can feel some of what I feel. You sense the great spans of time and the multitudinous worlds that I carry in my unfailing memory. You know that I've given and taken away life, many times. You sense the vengeful grief that suffuses me as we swim through higher and higher reaches, where the life-giving neighbourhoods have been replaced by fields of waste.

Once, we're swimming through a deep valley when we stumble upon a hill of bright yellow eggs, smooth like the shell I found you in, stacked up like a fort. Something sinister leaks from their innards.

Don't go near! Your voice is full of alarm. *Let's get out of here.*

We swim away. I'm simmering with anger. But I'm surprised when I realise that yours flared first, before mine. Your rage heats me from within.

Do you know who did this?

A quiver of guilt. *I came down here to find out more. To see things for myself. To try and change things.*

Can you?

You shake your head uncertainly. *I don't have much power.*

—

From time to time, you close your eyes and fall asleep. You've taken to wrapping your arms around mine when you sleep, so that you don't flop around. I think back to the moment I cracked your soft, strange, wormy form out of its silver shell and pondered what you were and whether you were poisonous. Now, a wash of blue tinges the skin beneath your eyes, as my blood rushes through your body. I know that when we jet along at high speeds, the curve of your mouth means you're enjoying yourself. I know that the taste of seaweed makes you shudder in disgust, and the taste of crab makes you shiver in pleasure.

Different things make your heart pound: when a shark's shadow passes over us, when you're angry with me for not shielding you from my torrent of thoughts, and, sometimes, when you're asleep, twitching with dreams or nightmares. I could dip into your subconscious. Some time ago, I wouldn't have cared. But now I refrain.

One day, I sense something different in you.
What's wrong? Are you dying?
You laugh—a pleasant chime reverberating up my arm. *No, the opposite.*
Oh?
I can hear parts of my mind I've never heard before. I can see the parts of me that were covered up. Did you do this to me?
Not intentionally.
Is your mind always like this?
My mind doesn't have hidden layers. My mind is like a mountain, out in the open. Yours is like a narrow valley, folded in the dark.
How frightening. You shiver.
To have a mind without layers?
To know yourself completely.

—

Another time, in the drowsiness of just-waking, you ask me whether I have a name.
I tell you that I have many, but no one uses them anymore.
Why not?
There's no need to. They all know who I am.
Well, did you have a mother?
A long, long time ago.
What did she call you?
She gave me her own name. Mother-of-the-trenches.
Right. When you look at me now, your disgust and fear is gone. *Well, Mother-of-the-trenches, it's a pleasure to meet you. I'm Tam.*

—

After a long time, we swim through new places. It's so bright here, so full of light it hurts my eyes, but we push on. We meet new creatures, smaller even than you, that clump together in multitudes, building a fortress from the skeletons of their ancestors. We pull out a piece of taint from where it's trapped in the reef and tuck it in the curl of an arm.

Where are we going? you ask, not for the first time.
I've decided to take you home.
Fear stabs through you. *No.*
But you want to go home.
No. You gesture at our conjoined bodies. *Not like this.*
Why not?
Are you mad? We're a freak show.

The whites of your eyes are veined with purple. I swell up to double my size. Fiery stripes flow over my skin. Several of my arms, of their own accord, rise above my head, thrusting the tainted debris aloft.

What does it matter? I say. *We are powerful.*

—

It's a sweltering January afternoon, and Bondi Beach is sardined with roasted bodies, sunburned shoulder to pruny buttock. When the swell first appears on the horizon, the surfers shout in glee. But as the wave approaches, the shouts become panicked screams. Boards collide and bodies tumble in a ragtag race to shore. Sunbathers leap to their feet, tripping over towels and umbrellas and sandcastles.

The tide rises. The wave soars. Behind it, there's a monstrous shape, blocking out the sky. As the beach empties, something breaks the ocean's surface. Gigantic tentacles writhe over an ancient, wrinkled head. A conglomeration of plastic garbage, fishing nets, sewage waste, animal corpses, and radioactive barrels pushes towards the shorefront.

Later, much later, the recollections of the survivors are fragmented and contradictory. Some described watching in horror as truck-sized tentacles flailed across the sand, flinging people into the sky. Some recalled being pelted by pieces of garbage and dead sea creatures. Some described, bizarrely, what seemed to be a half-formed human attached to the one of the monster's arms; skin shimmering blue, eyes burning with rage.

And there were a few who stood and watched the whole thing from start to finish, unable to move. They were consumed, they said, by the alien beauty of the creature rising from the depths. They spoke, with hushed awe, of rows of suckers with purple rims and pale centres, gleaming wetly in the sun, and of psychedelic skin, like worlds exploding. And those glittering eyes, they whispered, with pupils so deep and black they were invisible. Those eyes held a vengeful gravity, like the dark, devouring heart of a galaxy.

The Scent of Olives

Rob Porteous

Argos was walking very slowly. I could feel his fatigue through the harness. He was an old dog—much younger than me in years perhaps but, on baking hot summer days, we both felt very old.

He was hardly leading me anymore; it was more like I was pushing him. In truth, I hardly needed his guidance—we walked that way most days. I knew every uneven flagstone on the path.

We passed under the feathery shade of a tree and had a moment's respite from the sun. Argus didn't change his pace. He padded on, panting, keen to get to the shop and rest. There was the sound of shouting behind us, from further back up the street. Angry voices, drunk perhaps.

I walked a little faster.

We passed an alley to the left, the void marked by the sudden absence of reflected noise, the cool of its shadows. I counted a few more steps and we reached the shade of an awning. The clatter of an air conditioner and the smell of spiced meat confirmed we were in the right place.

Stepping into the chill of the air-conditioned shop was like wading into a pool of cool water. We both moved to our proper places. Argos went and sat down in a corner, on the tiles—one of the girls would bring him some water in a moment. I moved forward by myself, pacing out the distance to the counter, stopping with my hand on the cold glass of the vitrine.

Niko came from the back, calling out in his strong voice. "Theia Stheno! Kalimera, what a surprise to see you!"

It was no surprise. I was there, at Niko's Continental Foods, every other day.

"What will you have, Theia?"

Theia Stheno, Auntie Stheno—that's what Niko's father, Konstantinos, had called me. He and I had both ended up in Melbourne in '49, escaping from the Civil War, from the memories of war. Back then, while the rest of the world was celebrating the peace, Greece had returned to the abyss. We'd been lucky to get out. He started the shop—it was just a milk bar then, the Parthenon, but he'd sold proper food, real cheese and olives, from out the back to the other Greeks. Refugees from an uncivil war, we had to look after each other. All the older women were "Theia". Regardless of where in Greece we had come from, in Melbourne we became family.

Stheno, it meant strong. A long time ago, I'd lived up to my name, been proud of it even. But I'd come to Australia to put the memory of all that behind me. In Melbourne, we had needed to be strong in a different way, to cope with the loss of our loved ones, with the exile we had chosen. I wondered if Niko ever thought of what my name meant. Probably not. To him, it was just a name—I'd always been "Theia Stheno", from when he was born. With the years, I'd become old and frail, but he hadn't seemed to notice the irony.

"Theia?"

"Some kefalotyri, just a slice." I held up my thumb and forefinger to show how thick. I could smell a hint of goat's milk as he cut the cheese and put it on the scales to weigh it. It was aged, salty, as sharp as tears.

I'd had more in common with Konstantinos than being swept out of Greece on the tide of the exodus. The wars had taken his parents and a brother. I'd lost my youngest sister. Raped. Then killed by a soldier for "fraternising". My other sister was Euryale, the middle one. I'd brought Eury to Australia hoping it would help her to get away from the memories of the violence.

"And some olives." I didn't need to say what kind. Niko knew I'd only want the salt-cured sort, black and wrinkled, bathed in oil, like back home. There was a chink as he put a glass jar on the counter.

When we were young, Eury had always been the adventurous sister. But in the end, she'd been the one who hadn't been able to endure leaving our home. Perhaps she'd missed our other sister too much, as well. Either way, she just pined away.

I was the oldest. I'd never thought I would end up alone.

"That's all," I said.

"Would you like some dolmades? They're fresh, Chrys made them this morning."

Dolmades?

For a moment, I was transported back to when we were girls, cooking on an open fire under the olive trees. We'd boil goat meat in an iron pot until the flesh melted away from the bones, then throw in handfuls of wheat and fresh herbs, letting it simmer so the grain soaked up the juices. It would smell so good that we could hardly wait until it had cooled enough to let us use vine leaves to scoop out steaming handfuls of pungent, aromatic stew. We laughed and ate beneath the olive branches and the Ionian Sea sparkled far below, out to the wine-dark horizon.

I wrinkled my nose. But not *these* dolmades. Bland rice that tasted of nothing, wrapped in vine leaves as bitter as disappointment. Pah!

Niko sighed and I heard the rustle as he put my things into a plastic bag. I passed him my purse. He'd give me the right money back.

"I've put in some paximadia."

I called them dipyros, "twice-baked". The savoury rusks would be too hard for my teeth, but I could always dip them in a little water and vinegar to soften them. They'd be good with the cheese.

"S' efharistó," I thanked him. He wouldn't have charged for the dipyros.

He came around and put the bag in my hands. Argos stood and shook himself with a rattle, then walked over. I bent down and felt for the harness.

"Yiá sou!" Niko opened the door and we walked out, turning back along the way we'd come.

The heat outside hit me like walking into an oven. As we left the shade of the awning, I felt the force of the sun on my face. It was very quiet. There were no cars. I wondered what day of the week it was. Was it Sunday? No, it couldn't be; Niko's was shut on Sundays.

My black scarf and long black yiayia frock soaked in the sun. Maybe it was too hot even for cars. We should have come earlier.

We reached the alley and Argos stopped. I shook the harness irritably. Why was he stopping? I wanted to get home!

Then I heard footsteps, scuffing on the pavement—two people. They seemed to be right in front of me, blocking our path.

Argos was pushing me back, into the alley. He was trained not to growl, but he was growling now.

"Hey, lady. Can yah give us five bucks for the bus?" A young male voice, high pitched, nasal.

I shook my head. I took another step back and the rough brickwork rasped at my hand. The sudden pain was like a shock. I tried to back away further but bumped up against a rubbish skip—there was nowhere to go.

"Give us yah bag or you'll be sorry!" a second voice snarled. It was so close it startled me.

The nasal voice: "Oh Jeez, put the fuckin' knife away! She can't see it anyway, yah dumbfuck. Just get the bag!"

Snarler didn't want to give up. He'd just started. I could sense his excitement at my helplessness, my frailty. I stood jammed into the corner of the wall and the skip, holding my handbag to my chest like a shield, the shopping bag hanging down in front.

There was a sudden jerk as something slashed at the plastic shopping bag. The jar of olives smashed at my feet. Argos was barking angrily, further down the alley.

Snarler hooted with excitement. "Give us yer bag, granny, or you're next. I've got a knife, see?"

I didn't want any trouble. I'd seen too much in my life already. I loosened my hold on the handbag. They were only boys. If I gave them the money, they'd leave.

Argos was barking louder. Surely someone would hear.

"Shaddup, yah mangy cunt!" Argos yelped in pain. The Whiner must have kicked him. And again; Argos yipped, high-pitched, pain edged with terror.

No, this had to stop! I pulled at my glasses. They were tangled in my scarf and I tugged at them until they both came off.

Whiner screamed, "What the fuck?"

I opened my eyes. Whiner was a couple of steps away, already turning to run, mouth gaping in terror.

His eyes met mine. He was moving in desperate slow motion, like he was swimming in treacle. His face got paler.

Then he stopped.

I straightened from the stoop of long years as his life filled my lungs. I felt a surge of blood through withered legs and arms, painful . . . exhilarating, as the strength returned.

I flexed my fingers, feeling them limber up. There was a crackle of power.

I heard a blubbering moan at my feet. Snarler had fallen onto all fours. I could smell hot piss.

I took a step towards him. He scrambled to get away, crawling through the mess of olives and oil, slashing his hands on the shards of glass. He half turned, one arm stretched back, trying to keep me away with a bloodied palm.

Staring at me, eyes wide.

He mouthed a scream, but the sound was choked as his throat turned to stone. I waited for a moment, watching his colour fade, feeling the power in me double.

I hadn't felt so alive for aeons!

I moved past him to get to Argos. He was lying at Whiner's feet, his breath laboured. I pulled on Whiner's cold, white shoulder and toppled him onto the prone figure of Snarler. The bodies shattered into chalky rubble.

I knelt and stroked him, my loyal Argos.

"You'll be alright." I held out my hand. There were spots of blood where I'd grazed it on the wall. He licked them off, then pulled away, shaking himself. He clambered up, bobbing his head from side to side, suddenly almost skittish. He barked once, loudly. He sounded strong again.

Squatting there, I breathed in the scent of olives and the limey smell of freshly broken stone. I looked up at a pure white cloud, caught in the strip of bright sky framed by the alley. Galanolefci—white on blue, the Greek flag.

Greece, but not Greece.

I remembered the skies of home, remembered my sisters, Euryale . . . and poor, murdered Medusa.

The serpents in my hair hissed and writhed, stretching for the light. They yearned for the sun.

My heart was thumping. It too yearned. It yearned for blood, for the old ways of killing.

Argos nuzzled my hand, wanting to go home. Absent-mindedly, I scrabbled my fingers between his ears.

I went back and picked up my glasses, then unknotted my scarf and tied it back on, pushing the unruly snakes back into place. I stood, brushing my skirts straight and closed my eyes.

I was exiled, but this land had brought me peace. After so many years, maybe I owed it as much in return.

"Come, Argos. We go home."

Bruises Black and Blue

Leife Shallcross

The night she came to me, my underwater world was all indigo shadows and spilled-milk moonlight. She crashed through the mirror-black surface in a fever of gilded bubbles and hung for a moment, an arrested phantom amid the billows of her gown, before slowly sinking down into the unmoving depths.

I watched her fall, head first. I waited as she settled into the soft, cold mud, raising a gentle cloud of pond muck, like a silent sigh. Her arms took a little longer to come to rest among the strands of rank grass and empty snail shells, and her hair took the longest of all, a drifting veil of ragged black silk, shrouding her face.

When all was still, I uncoiled and slid through the silt to investigate this new gift. At first, I only looked. Circling around her, my limbs held close against my body, propelling myself with just my tail. I skimmed past one outstretched leg, laid bare amid the settling folds of fabric. Over an outflung hand, the half-curled fingers inert. Eventually, I came to a stop by her head, digging my long, narrow toes into the mud and sinking down to squat beside her. She was so young. I reached out with webbed fingers to smooth a horde of tiny bubbles from where they hid amongst the tresses of her hair and sent them scurrying upwards like a school of tiny, iridescent fish. Her eyes were open. One last breath lingered, limned in silver, trapped between her lips. It was her throat, though, that told me as much of her story as I needed to know. Her throat, wound with its necklace of bruises. Blooms of sapphire, onyx and amethyst just visible under white skin.

I ran my tongue between my needle teeth. There was meat, here. Juicy and dark, ripe for the plucking. Bones for cracking and marrow for sucking. *But* . . . Perhaps there was more. I wound myself around her, unwrapping her with great delicacy and perfect patience. I peeled her apart, painstakingly unfolding pleats and convolutions, investigating cavities and declivities, wondering over the cryptic ciphers of her capillaries, the plump and gleaming bounty of her viscera. And there, caged within the ivory architecture at her core, I found it. The key. Ruby red and hot to touch, shot through with shining veins of grief and glass-sharp terror. Her last plea. Her last hope. Vicious and pure. Crystallised as her throat was crushed and her breath died, and she fell slowly down to me. I handled it carefully. I plucked it free and that last silver swallow of air broke from her lips and swam upwards. When it broke the surface, all those within a league would have heard her anguished wail.

—

I made her up anew. It took me the waning and waxing of a moon to have her ready. She lay so long in my bower all her colours leached away. When she was almost done, I gave her a necklace to replace the collar of blue bruises she'd worn to her death. Pearls fit for a queen. I made them myself. I searched amongst my watery ossuary for the teeth of murdered women and rolled them between my palms until they became smooth and round. I wrapped them in silver fish scales until they gleamed and wound them all about her slender neck. Then I took her heart in my hands and parted her lips and crawled inside. And we were one.

—

Who, at the moment of their birth, knows themselves for who they are? Not I, never I. No matter how many times I venture this course. Each time I am reborn to my task, I awake in a tangle of unfamiliar limbs, my head full of memories pulped together, some formless and intangible, some with wicked edges. Picking out the ones that are mine, and the ones that aren't but that make sense, the ones I can use, is like fishing splinters of bone out of freshly shucked marrow.

That night I knew only the weight of water, the tearing pain of breath through waterlogged flesh. A wracking cough and sour spume on my tongue. I woke sprawled in a puddle, my body a strange-familiar configuration of ungainly limbs. Rain fell in ragged gusts all around me. I was on a path amongst trees. I sat up and pushed aside the long strands of hair plastered against my cheek. One of my feet was bare. On the other was a crumpled stocking and a sodden slipper. I wore a dress so colourless, it was as though I had lain out in the weather for weeks.

Then my eyes fell upon a great, dark pool a dozen paces away. The torrents of rain had filled it brimful and more. The sight of that dark water, creeping out of its depthless hole and across the ground towards me, reassured me. Even curled up tight within this fragile cage of meat and bone, I was not powerless. I staggered to my borrowed feet and stumbled away, into the trees.

—

The path was fingerbone-pale and certain as fate, pointing the way through a world filled with wind and water and thrashing trees. Following it was the only thing to do, even as it grew rocky and narrow. When it went up, I went up with it. When it left the trees behind, the wind grew worse, tearing at me and flinging my hair in my face.

The path became a series of stone steps. I stumbled upwards until they ended and I could go no further. Above me, and to either side, a stone wall stretched into the tumultuous darkness. What to do? It took me some time, picking through the tangled skeins of borrowed memory before I found the knowledge I needed: as good as blind with wind and darkness, I groped at the wall before me until I felt rough wood. The door was set into a shallow recess and my first instinct was to huddle against it, out of the driving misery of the weather. I let my weary legs fold and sank down onto the step.

I felt another memory glimmer faintly under the surface of her fading mind. Had she come through this door once? Perhaps in daylight, when the world was green and soft. *Perhaps it was another door.* But doors could open and there might be shelter on the other side. I raised my fist and pounded upon the ironbound timber, as hard as I could. The wind tore the feeble sounds of my knocking away, but I tried again, not knowing what else to do.

I heard a muffled oath and footsteps.

"Who's there?" called a rough voice.

I did not know how to answer that question.

"Please," I cried "Have mercy!"

For a moment I feared my words would go unheard, lost in the rush of wind. Then there came another oath, and the door opened. I toppled in over the doorstep, bringing water and cold air with me.

"Mother of God!" said the voice, above me now. Sprawled across the flagstones, my dripping hair hanging in my eyes, I could only see his boots.

"Please, have mercy," I said again, turning my face up to see my saviour.

He hesitated, crossing himself, but when I did nothing more alarming than stare pitifully up at him, he bent over and helped me to my feet.

"Hands like ice." he muttered to himself. He stepped back quickly and stood looking at me with the scrutiny of one assessing a possible threat. "Who are you?" His face set faint chords of familiarity ringing in my acquired memories.

"Please," I whispered. I looked down at myself.

My dress had once been fine, but was now sodden and muddy. My feet were bare, soiled and bloody, my remaining slipper having been lost somewhere along the path. Something gleamed beneath my chin and I put my hand up to my throat. *Ah. The pearls.* There was a memory all my own. I touched them and the water ran down off me, gathering in dark puddles at my feet.

"Can you walk?" he asked.

I nodded.

—

I trailed after him. There were dark corridors and greasy yellow lanterns. I thought how much more pleasing this castle might be, filled with water, festooned with ribbons of weed unfurling in gentle currents and lit with the gentle aquamarine glow of shoals of bloodworm spawn.

The ill-lit hallways ended at another door. This door held something in, something growling and murmuring, an energy that spilled sharp orange light through the cracks. My escort pounded upon it and for a moment a terror gripped me at what lay beyond. Then it burst open and I saw it was only more light and a very great many people, all talking and calling out and laughing together. Little by little, those closest to me turned to look at me and fell silent, a pool of quiet spreading out around me and into the hall. The wave of it ran forward and lapped at the feet of the high table until they noticed me too.

"What is the meaning of this?"

A man stood up at the high table, grey-haired, but broad-shouldered and broad-girthed under a velvet doublet of midnight blue. Beside him sat a woman in a gown of periwinkle silk, rich with gilded embroideries and scattered with winking jewels. She was not so old as her lord, but old enough to be mother to the youth who sat on his other side and the young women who sat a little further along. Her gaze was as sharp and careful as an expertly wielded knife and it came to rest upon the pearls at my throat.

"A waif, came knocking upon the postern gate," said the man who had let me in.

"She's no waif," whispered the lady, still staring at my pearls.

The young man said nothing, but glared at me with an expression so tangled and thorny I felt something inside me begin to uncurl.

The lady leaned towards the lord and whispered something in his ear.

"Give her food," he said sharply. Perhaps he meant a servant, but it was the beautiful young man with the murderous expression who moved. He brought me his own plate, piled with a half-eaten meal. The burned meat I had no stomach for, browned and stinking as it was. I like my meat fresh and flavoured with the blood that gave it life. Instead I took an indigo plum from his plate. My borrowed teeth were square and blunt and skidded over the surface of the plumskin before breaking through into the flesh. He watched me suck on the stone and lick my fingers clean.

"What happened to you?" he hissed so that only I could hear. "What happened to your hair?"

I touched the sodden strands hanging about my face, lifting one to where I could see it. The damp hair clung to my finger, moon-pale.

"Please," I whispered. "Have mercy."

He went white, the blood draining from his face in an instant. Then he turned on his heel and strode back to the table without another word.

The lady's knife-keen gaze had not left me. She lifted a hand.

"A hot bath for our guest," she instructed. "I will oversee her bed. Come, my dear." She stood and left the table, coming close to me. She lifted her eyes from my throat to my face. "We will look after you," she said.

—

She led me up a flight of steps so steep and tall my borrowed legs ached dully before I reached the top. We passed two doors; she opened a third and I followed her inside. For a moment I thought she had somehow brought me to the bottom of a well. The room was round and lined with stones, and when I raised my eyes the ceiling was painted indigo and set with gilded stars. But dry air still rasped through my borrowed throat and crackled in my lungs. She stood in the doorway, watching me as I gazed up at the false stars.

"You are so pale, child," she murmured, her gaze moving from my face to my throat and back again. "You look half dead. Let us take care of you." Then she clapped her hands and servants bustled around us. First, they brought a tub and lined the sides with soft cloth, then they filled it with buckets of water, gently steaming and smelling of summer. When it was half-full, two women came to take my clothes. I did not let them remove the pearls.

"What's this then?" asked one of the women, lifting my hand. My fingers were curled closed. She eased them open. In my hand was the plum stone. "I'll put this here, shall I?" she said, placing it on a low table by the bed. Her voice was light, but I saw the looks that passed between her and the other women around me. Curiosity. Wariness. Pity. Fear.

I sat in the tub while they prepared my bed, letting the song of the water creep under my skin. Under the ghostly fragrance of the flowers floating about my knees and the wild scent of the rain still clinging to my hair, I could discern the mineral tang of the stones of the well from which the bathwater had been drawn. Eventually, however, a note of agitation in the murmuring of the servants filtered through my languor. The lady stood by the door, directing a parade of women carrying armfuls of bolsters and blankets and pillows into the room. I frowned. They had not prepared me a bed so much as built me a tower of mattresses, looming over our heads in the centre of the room.

"My lady," asked one of the older women, "are you sure?"

"Look how delicate she is," said the lady. "We must see her comfortable."

At last they came to help me from my bath and I stood still while they dried me, blotting each drip of water from between my fingers and my toes, patting at the pearls and combing out the sodden strands of my alabaster hair.

"She's so pale," said the older servant.

"Like a lily," said the lady softly. "Or a pearl. Flawless." Her gaze moved again, from the pearls resting against my naked skin, up to my face. She smiled. She continued to watch as my flawless pallor was covered with a nightgown of linen so fine the candlelight showed through it. Then she took my hands and kissed my cheeks and led me to the ladder they had set against the towering bed so that I might climb up to the top. She helped me up the steps and when I was settled, she climbed up to draw the covers over me herself.

"Rest well, my dear," she said. "I hope you will be comfortable here. We will talk again in the morning."

I could almost have laughed as she led the procession of serving-women out of my room. Talk *again?* I had said three words since I entered these halls! What, I wondered, made her think I had anything further to say?

I lay quietly in the dark for the longest time. Despite the veritable castle they had constructed for my repose, I was not comfortable. The sense of being at the bottom of a well might have been reassuring but for the stilted stars in their unsettlingly ordered ranks above me. And there was something else. Like a stone in a shoe, or an unwelcome growth under the skin. A tiny, intractable presence pushing at me, encroaching on the space I took up in the world. It was, I began to realise, the faintest thread of a spell. It was not a strong one, or, at least, it was not strong enough to bind *me*. But it made me curious. I slid out from under the covers and went back down the ladder. There, on the table where the kind servant had put my plum stone, a gift given to me by the house, was nothing but a candlestick holding a snuffed-out candle. I smiled.

And, beyond my chamber door, a noise.

My smile grew.

The door handle creaked and began to slowly turn. I waited.

The door inched open slowly. A pale hand curled around it, easing it open further. A figure stepped inside, an inkblot shadow with hard, glittering edges. His sapphire eyes caught a stray shaft of moonlight as he saw me standing by the bed. He closed the door as softly and carefully as he had opened it, then surged across the room towards me. I did not even have time to gasp before he grabbed me by the throat and shoved me back against the wall of mattresses.

"What are you doing here?" he hissed into my face. "What happened to you?"

Instinct surged and I tried to speak, but the pressure of his hand cut off the flow of air that gave me voice and all I could do was open and close my jaw uselessly. It hardly mattered. I'd said all I had to say to him already.

He grabbed a fistful of my hair and dragged at it.

"What happened to your hair? Where did you get those pearls? *Why are you here?*"

He held me pinned and mute.

What to do? His thirst for violence rolled off him in murky clouds and I could not afford to have this fragile cage of mine broken beyond repair. Not yet. Then from deep in the complicated creases of the dead girl's torpid mind I spied a useful memory, glimmering like a lost jewel. I lifted my hands and twined them around his neck, pulling him close. He gasped in shock, then began to thrash as though *he* was the caught fish. He slammed against me, shoving me into the unyielding softness at my back. Somewhere inside myself I coiled and coiled, holding myself back, willing those frail hands to keep hold of him, until he groaned—a ragged surrender of a sound—and slumped forward, his face pressing into the tower of bolsters. His grip on my throat loosened and I crumpled quietly at his feet.

He put his hand on my head, gentle this time.

"See what you do to me?" he whispered, accusing and tender all at once. Then: "Why did you come back?"

I waited.

Suddenly, he snatched his hand back as though I burned him. He jerked back a step.

"*How?*" he rasped out. "How did you come back?"

"Please," I whispered into the darkness swelling between us. "Have mercy."

He made a sound as though someone had hit him. A moment later he was stumbling away from me and out of my room, his movements frantic.

I dragged myself onto unsteady feet and crossed the room to close the door noiselessly behind him. Then I made my way back up the ladder and under the blankets of the bed his mother had built for me, aching from where his body had beat at the one I wore.

But I smiled in the dark as I pressed my fingers into those newly tender places. Oh, the bruises I would have come morning.

—

The serving women who came to tend me the next day clucked and fluttered around me as much as I could have wished. They called for the lady in their distress. I stood before her, once again a naked, wilting lily. Only this time I was clearly despoiled, blooms of black and blue and mulberry marking the soft, white skin of my back and belly. She looked at me, a frown on her forehead and a spark of something uncertain in her eyes, the first two fingers of one hand pressed to her lips.

"I don't understand," whimpered the kindly woman from the night before. "Who could have harmed her?"

The lady did not seem to expect me to respond. Instead she turned her face away and whispered something in her serving-woman's ear. The woman's eyes grew wide and round.

"Bring her clothes," commanded the lady. "She must be dressed like the lady she surely is to bruise so easily through twenty feather mattresses."

I was fussed and fretted over, and eventually led from my chamber gowned in a sumptuous dress of forget-me-not blue and palest gold that lay heavy on my smarting skin. I broke my fast with the lady and her daughters in her private chambers, eating a handful of grapes and some newly shelled hazelnuts. I refused the bread and cooked meat.

After that, there was nothing more but to submit to the languid industry that made up the minutiae of a fine lady's day. I had nothing much to offer. The gossamer memories in my borrowed brain suggested I had once taken pride in spinning and sewing, but these fingers remembered nothing of those arts now. I could not even contribute to the conversation with the only three words allowed me. The lady tried. She asked me about my mother and father and my home, and if I could recall how I came to be lost on their lands. All I could do was look back into her hopeful face and shake my head sorrowfully. She was the consummate hostess all the same, and effortlessly smoothed over my deficit of conversation with anecdotes and observations of her own. I was thankful for it. I could slide away inside myself, away from the monotony of her luxuriously appointed parlour, and imagine myself back in my beloved depths. While she and her women discussed the reckoning of the castle accounts, I recalled teaching the elvers to wind and hide amongst the rocks. While the women debated what medicines needed to be stocked against the coming winter, I lost myself in memories of chasing glinting fish through filtered sunshafts and of sucking on the lithe and transparent bones of the slowest.

So passed the time until her son came to sit with us over the midday meal. Then I had something to truly entertain myself with.

"My lady," he asked, offering me a plate of figs, his manner as smooth and charming as his mother's.

I lowered my face demurely and looked up at him through lashes leached as pale as sun-aged bone.

"Please," I said softly.

He froze. His eyes went wide, his pupils huge and dark. He looked as though he was waiting for a blow. I took a fig and tore it open.

—

That night I let myself be tempted by an oyster, raw and plump with salty juice. I carefully licked the pearly shell clean and tucked it into my pocket, knowing it would find its way under my mattresses while I was readied for bed by the swarm of serving women. Later, when I lay alone in the dark, I could feel it digging away at me, next to the plum stone, but this time I did not get out of bed.

Of course, the son visited me again that night. I rolled into a stray moonbeam illuminating the edge of my colossal bed and watched him close the door as silent as a snake. This time he locked it. These borrowed eyes could not see in the dark so well as my own, but I could see enough. He stood at the bottom of the ladder, his face turned up towards me. I leaned the pale beacon of my moonlit face on my chin and looked down at him.

"Won't you come down?" he whispered. "Then we can talk."

I waited.

"Come now," he said, "it would not be seemly for me to come up there."

I waited. His breath grew uneven.

"You are not being fair," he hissed. "Why do you make me like this?"

"Please." It may have come out a little mocking.

He surged up the ladder. I had to clench my teeth to hide my grin.

When he pushed me down I did not resist. I could feel his hands on my collarbone, his knee between my thighs, the plum stone and the oyster shell pressing into the small of my back.

"Is this what you want?" he snarled.

"Have mercy," I choked out, past the weight of his elbow in the hollow of my throat.

He kissed me, putting his mouth over mine savagely, as though he was trying to swallow me up. Inside my cage I readied myself. A gurgle surged up my throat. It could have been either rage or laughter. He reared back, his face pale and shocked in the darkness.

"You're so cold!" he choked. He let go of me abruptly, scrubbing at his mouth with his sleeve. He scrabbled back away from me, tangling in the bedclothes.

"Please?" I begged him. I reached out my hands towards him. Fruit was unfulfilling and one oyster would never be enough. He lashed out with his feet, kicking me away, his feet connecting with all the soft, unprotected places of my belly.

"Have—" I gasped.

"Stop saying that!" he cried hoarsely.

I let him go and he fled, half-falling down the ladder, stumbling across my chamber in the dark.

—

The next morning, the serving women did not cluck. They did not flutter. They uttered low cries and drew back, faces bloodless with fear. The lady was called again.

"What can it mean?" they asked each other, unable to look away from the bruises mottling my belly.

The lady inspected me gently.

"Do not frighten her," she scolded her women, her hands resting upon my bare shoulders. "It is a trick of chance. You will convince her there is some evil afoot where all I see is superstitious peasants wailing! You, there! Bring me a compress of witch hazel and comfrey."

The murmurs subsided but did not cease. Because it was true. The awful mottling of bruises across my torso did indeed look remarkably like an enormous frog, sprawled against my white skin. Or a toad. Or something else, squat and mottled, that lurked in damp places and liked its meat fresh.

—

They caught me in nets of gossamer and laced me into ells of ocean-blue brocade. I sailed, cumbersome in my skirts, on a tide of whispering, suspicious women through corridors of soulless stone to the lady's boudoir. And there I sat, amidst the wash of murmurs and the gentle buffeting of sideways glances for the time it took the sun to cross the sky and begin to sink into the western horizon. I watched a snail make its way up a window pane, leaving the barely-there shimmer of its journey behind it. I watched a cobweb waft and billow against a draught. There was music, which annoyed me. And the lady spoke eagerly about the richness of her husband's lands, which bored me. Her daughters recited their catechism and her son came to visit, but he did not try to offer me food this time. He sat a little too far away and smiled with cruelly barbed charisma, but his eyes would not stay upon me, sliding off like raindrops from lily pads.

—

There was another storm that night. The castle kept it at bay with music and dancing. The lady appointed herself my keeper and bestowed my hand to selected supplicants. I let myself be stepped in slow circles and paraded up and down by a dozen different men. But the son of the house stayed up at the high table, watching me hungrily with his dark blue eyes.

"You see," he whispered furiously to me between dances, "your enchantment wanes. You cannot lure me into—"

"Please," I whispered back at him; quiet, beseeching. I placed the tips of two fingers on the pearls wound around my oh-so-slender throat. "Have mercy."

He choked on his wine and did not speak to me again.

The lady heard him splutter and a little crease appeared between her eyes.

—

That night I ate some roasted fowl and kept the thighbone. I did not enjoy the dull, stringy meat, but I could *just* taste an echo of the quiet, tannin-stained lake the bird had lived on. The thighbone was gone brittle with heat and the press of it through the pile of feather mattresses was more uncomfortable than either the plum stone or the oyster shell. I wondered if I had miscalculated in letting the lady collect it. Were three tokens enough? None alone were strong enough to bind me, but together? I did not think so, but . . . No matter. I had always intended it to be tonight.

I lay, curled in my cage of cold flesh and brittle bone, looking out into the dark and listening to the keening of my dead girl's wounded heart. All the pain and terror, all the rage she had brought with her down to my bower were still there. But now a new thread ran through it. Or perhaps something old was swelling back into life. Had the mother's small magics called it up? Some disused conduit in that pulsing, red core, crushed and drained, now ran with a glimmer of renewed vitality. She'd loved him once. I sighed and her ribcage heaved. Such ichor was a sticky poison, but familiar.

I held myself ready, waiting for him to come. This time, though, instead of my door opening in sly silence, I heard voices.

"Don't! Don't!"

"Go back to bed, Mother. This has nothing to do with you!"

"You don't need to do this! You will have her, I swear! Just wait one more day—"

He cut her off with a laugh.

"I've heard about the bruises, Mother. How do *you* think she got them?"

"A binding sometimes holds too hard—" The lady's voice was muffled by the door and broken by her guilt.

She thought her petty magic had harmed me!

I pushed back the covers and began to climb down the ladder. He laughed again and said something too low for me to hear.

"No!"

There was a scuffle and a shocked, feminine cry. The door flew open as I reached the floor. He stood there, dark against the dark, his shoulders hunched in anger. The lady was crumpled in a heap behind him.

"Stop!" she moaned. "You don't have to do this! I have bound her."

He laughed. "Whatever for? Don't let those pearls fool you, mother. I don't know where she got them, but she is not some lost princess."

The lady sobbed and I stood up straight as he surged through the dark towards me. He grabbed at my bleached hair and pulled my head back.

"Now you'll give me that kiss you promised me," he snarled.

I didn't say anything. I opened my borrowed mouth.

He leaned over me and sealed his lips over mine.

I opened her mouth wider.

One of his hands dragged at my hair. The other dug bruising fingers into my shoulder.

Now.

Deep in her shell, her heart pulsed where I cradled it.

No! it wailed, not unexpectedly. And *No!* again, more strongly, for a host of entirely different reasons. Her heart bled grief, her misspent love searing my skin inside her skin, but it was merely a few drops. Her grief for her own lost life and for the building misery that led to her end was richer and more plentiful by far. It gave me strength.

I uncurled and surged upwards. Her throat swelled as I passed through it. The string of pearls broke and went bouncing, chattering, across the stone-flagged floor.

I swallowed his frightened yell as I met his mouth with my *true* mouth and began to peel off my dying shell. He tried to pull away, of course, but I had caught him fast. He struggled beautifully, but in vain. I had to hang on as he thrashed against me; easing my mouth over his head as I eased out of hers. Behind him, his mama was screaming.

My hands came free of the skin I sloughed and I began to tear at his clothes, my claws shredding the inconvenient fabric. *Meat*, I craved *meat*, and I did not want it shrouded in linen and wool. I would be picking *that* out of my teeth for a month. He fell and I followed him down. His struggles began to weaken.

"No! No, no no!"

A rush of fabric washed past me. I swivelled my eyes to see what was afoot, even as I began to work my tongue into an eye socket. He twitched and shuddered.

It was the mother. She was thrusting her hand deep under the bottom-most mattress grasping desperately for one of her paltry tokens. Of course, she drew out the thighbone. She held it up towards me, muttering. I felt a momentary pulse of weakness, a vague inclination to draw back from the rich red taste of him. But my promise to the dead girl was stronger. I slithered a little further out of my discarded skin, gripping my prize and digging my tongue in a little further. His eyeball burst between my teeth. The juice was obscenely good.

"Leave him be!" panted the lady. Her face was white with horror and she exuded her own flood of useless love, the cloying sweetness turned bitter with fear.

Why do these mortals love? I wondered, watching her warily as she shook her charmed bone at me. Every dead woman who'd ever found her way down to me had nursed her own curdled pot of it like goblin treasure, turned rotten in the light of the sun. It had no useful purpose I could see. What did she think she could do for him now? As if to illustrate my point, my questing tongue found the soft succulence of his brain and with one last, deep convulsion, he died.

I kicked off the dregs of my borrowed skin, leaving berry-red smears across the flagstones. The lady took a step back as I stood, dragging up my catch. I could hear far off voices growing closer.

"Leave him," she begged me, choking on tears. "Leave him for me."

I drew his ruined head from my mouth.

"He was promised to me," I told her. "By the one who summoned me as he killed her. He is mine."

"His bones," she sobbed. "Please, give me his bones. I could make of them a decent burial."

I considered this.

"Perhaps," I conceded. I never could refuse the plea of a grief-broken woman. There were footsteps running in the corridor, though, so I dragged the limp weight of him up over my shoulders and stalked to the window. I turned back and nodded at the nasty little thigh bone in her hand. "Burn that in a month and throw the ashes into the wind. They'll show you where to find them."

She made a broken sound and fell to her knees, clutching the bone to her chest. I threw open the window and let the wind-tossed water sweep in, lending me its strength and fury. I grinned out into the wild, blue-black night.

Behind me, the doorway suddenly filled with shouting people. I sank my claws into the spoils of my dead girl's vengeance and leaped out into the storm. I hoped the lady would have the sense to gather up the pearls I'd left behind. They'd make a useful gift for a daughter. They'd tell her the kind of things a girl should know.

New Things

Joanne Anderton

SHE FOLLOWED BROKEN train tracks to the factory. It was slow going. With her heart almost spent, she worked on the smallest reserves, quarantining energy for higher functions rather than wasting it on speed. Not that this was her choice. The deepest drives of her programming impelled her to survive. Her shuddering body shed parts with each step, so much of herself discarded on the side of the road. But still, she walked, moderate step after moderate step, right to the factory gates.

And this one was not in ruin.

"Dammit," she hissed through cracked teeth. "Blast and darn it." And wished her designers had installed a more creative speech matrix.

For so long, she'd been searching for a workshop like this one. The files in her head were long out of date, and all the other factories she'd tried had turned out to be dust and debris. With her failing heart spitting like water on coals, she'd allowed herself a moment of hope that she might finally cease to function. And be free.

But now, as her hand wrapped itself around weakening steel, hope crumbled like rust in her palm. With a sudden burst of strength, she tore the gate from its hinges and tossed it away. Her legs carried her inside, where it was so dark her body was forced to donate extra energy to her eyes. Her heart gave a protesting flicker, a small lick of flame that tickled her ribcage.

Sight came slowly, revealing a large room full of her sisters: seemingly-endless rows of their limp and dangling bodies strung up from the ceiling. Naked and not yet combat fitted, they were shells with empty chests, smooth carbon-weave limbs and lidless eyes that could not close, but had never opened.

A basic retrieval program kicked in and, unable to stop herself, she began harvesting. She tore the back of the head off the closest sister and fitted it to her own. It was easier to replace an entire leg than fix the casing on her right thigh. A new finger here, a bronchial tube there, an eye plucked out and swapped, she made her way to the elevator shaft, fixing herself as she went.

When she reached it, her desperate programming hooked fingers around deteriorated cables and stepped over the edge. She slid down an empty shaft of windows and steel, past frozen robot arms, banks of dead crops, and empty chairs around empty tables in empty rooms. The cables ripped fresh scars into her newly-repaired hands, but did not snap, no matter how she silently wished them to. She landed on weak legs, then used the pipes along the walls to haul herself towards a room her databases insisted was the reactor.

But when she got there the lights were not burning, the dials were immobile, the consoles and screens dim. A great circular window was cut into the far wall, and on the other side the core hunched in shadows. At the centre of any reactor was its core, where hearts like hers were forged and extracted. But they were not supposed to be like this.

She slumped across the closest console, wiped dust from the dials and poised her fingers over switches, ready to reawaken the core, ready to harvest her heart, but . . .

Her hands stilled. She had no data on how to do so. Her processors floundered, sending queries to satellites they knew weren't there, digging into the deepest recesses of her own backup files. Nothing.

How could she not know?

Her programming panicked. It sent inane queries to all the microprocessors scattered throughout her body. It dredged file after file, memory after memory, every new piece of information ever learned from her sisters, every old byte of knowledge she was first loaded with. They played in front of her eyes but nothing told her how to restart a reactor. The data simply weren't there.

"We were never supposed to need it," she said, as her body dragged itself across the floor. "It's dead." She collapsed against the window, her fingers tapping a last-ditch rhythm on the reinforced glass. "And so are we."

Finally, she would be free.

Then a single bulb flickered into life behind her. And it lit a dial with a fluttering needle that quivered just above zero. And as the light slowly spread, activating switches, illuminating screens, a low groan rattled the window. And on the other side, the core moved.

It did not look the way a core should. Where were the carbon-fibre pressure tubes, interleaved with arteries in its long neck? Where were the moderator chains, forged from meteorite silver, binding its clipped wings? The virgin girls in hazsuit white, drenching iridescent scales in coolant? And the chest, pried open to expose a heart, chipped down to the coals?

What she saw instead was small and hunched and grey. It opened a single eye, looked right at her, and spoke, "No." Though not with its mouth. She felt that voice, rather than heard it.

"No," she replied, in turn. Because her heart leapt at the silent sound of that impossible voice, and her programming rallied. Feeling returned to her legs and inch by jerking inch her body forced itself to stand.

"I know why you are here." The core's voice was the heat of an unwanted heartbeat. "But there's not much of me left. What use could you make of this weakened heart?"

"I wouldn't take it, if I had the choice." Her body headed for the centre console and its newly-awakened screens. It opened access panels, dug a cable out of her arm, and connected itself manually. The prerogatives that drove her and what was left of the reactor that regulated the core spoke to each other directly. They kept her out of the loop.

As the machinery came back online, the lights in the core's containment brightened too. She saw now its scales were a faded red, and etched with old, thick scars. Its chest was wedged open by thick control rods drilled into the bones of its ribcage. Its heart, within, was an ember balanced in a dark void.

Her programming flicked some invisible switch, and machinery unfurled from within the walls of the core's containment. Arms and tubes, trays and screens, even a small console that dropped from the ceiling and crashed to the floor.

"This machine is old and out of use," the core said. "Your efforts to revitalise it may be futile." A hook sprung out of the wall near its chest and jabbed at the core's scales. "And painful."

She couldn't see what damage, if any, the hook was doing. "I do not understand pain," she said. "But I am sorry to see you trapped." She was struggling to articulate a concept, a feeling, at the very edge of her design. "Like me."

The core shuddered its wings and she caught the glimmer of silver moderators. "Do you have a name?" it asked.

"We are given no names."

"Do you have one you gave yourself, then?"

She opened her mouth but she did not have the language.

The core released a low sigh into her silence. "That was too much to hope for, I suppose."

As they spoke, the machinery in the walls was grinding to a halt. Metal screeched against metal, rusted arms kicked out, petulant and useless.

"If you do not take my heart," the core said. "You will die."

"I would cease to function without it," she replied. "But only something that is alive can die."

"Take it as a metaphor."

"I'm not sure I understand."

Another sigh. "You would prefer to cease functioning than to take what's left of my heart?"

She'd seen humans nod in agreement, and longed to do the same, but was lucky enough to have control over her voice. "The world above is empty. My sisters are gone. There are no missions, no targets. What am I for, now?"

"Empty?" The core shook itself, setting off a momentary spike in the dials. "I was asleep for longer than I realised."

Her body disconnected itself from the console and wavered, indecisive. The reactor was active again, but the hardware had deteriorated too far to do its job. So now what? Her self-preservation programming was not great at improvisation.

"The reactor that contains you isn't working," she informed the core. "My processors have exhausted all options, and found no new viable solution. I cannot take your heart."

"Then I am trapped. When you cease all function, I will be here. When you are nothing but rust and biometric mould, I will still be here. All alone. You raised a good question earlier, little killing bot. What are we even for?"

A good question. If she could have closed her eyes to think better about it, she would have. She was hardly designed for independent thought, but she was designed to learn. It was one of her main directives. She and her sisters were supposed to gather new information, and share it on their filial network. It made them more efficient, more adaptable.

"Why survive, when no one else has?" the core continued. "Why do I still burn, if I cannot fly? Even as a reactor core I had a purpose, chained and tortured though I may have been. But this? This is . . . this is . . ."

"Sad." The word felt strange. "It is . . . sad. No, it makes *me* . . . sad."

The core shifted again, closer to the window. "What use does a killing machine have of sad?"

A good question. She wanted to understand what the core was saying, she wanted to give it her opinion in reply. Wasn't that a kind of learning? Her programming wasn't convinced, but grudgingly handed her enough autonomy to shake her head. "I do not wish to leave you alone, trapped. As I have been. It makes me sad that I will."

That was certainly new. So that was certainly learning. She requested more processing power to analyse and file. Her programming had no choice but to give it.

"We cannot both be free. One of us will be trapped by what's left of my heart." The core's pulse skipped a beat, and she felt it in the flutter of her own. "Can you come closer?"

She tested her feet, and was surprised to find them responsive. She managed to shuffle to the window.

"You are correct," the core said. "You are not alive. You were created to wage a war you do not even understand. What does it matter if you feel sad for me? Your newly-found empathy cannot undo the atrocities done by your kind. So why do I care whether I condemn you to some hellish new eternity? Answer me that, little killing machine. Why do I care?"

Why do I care? A good question. More power needed. More handed over.

"I cannot answer."

"No, you cannot." The core's great face was so close to the glass. "I feel you slowing, I know that you are almost gone. Soon, nothing but inert coal will remain in your chest. I am running out of time. I have to decide."

"Decide what?"

"Whether something that was never alive can truly suffer."

In preparation for shutdown, her processors were running back through the events of the day, preparing to upload. There was nothing left to upload to, but the process was automatic.

She noticed something in the recap, and discovered she could hit pause. "You asked me if I have a name. Do you?"

"No human has ever known my name; no human could understand it." The core hesitated. "But of course, you are not one. Then tell me, can't you hear it?"

"My ears pick up all frequencies," she said. "But you make no sound."

"Can't you feel it?"

"My skin is a carbon-fibre weave designed to withstand high levels of damage. I do not feel."

"And yet we can speak, so I know you hear me."

"But that's through . . ." Her heart.

And as soon as she realised it, she could hear it. Something wordless whispered in flame, impossible and unprogrammable, and yet she understood. She listened, it filled her, flooded her, it was fire and air and rage and love and so many things she didn't have the language to categorise. She couldn't say how long she stood there, slumped against the window, while the core told her its name. For only a heartbeat? But finally, gradually, it faded.

And she waited a moment longer to reassemble her fragmented thoughts before she replied, "I cannot call you that."

The core snorted something like a laugh, and tiny puffs of smoke rose from its mouth. She realised it had teeth. She wondered what a core ate, or if they were purely decorative, like hers. So many new things to learn.

"And yet you asked. Let us make a deal, Nameless. In this deal, I will trust you. And in this deal, you will reward my trust. Do you agree?"

She gave it what consideration she could. "I have never been trusted before. Because I can only behave within certain parameters, it is a given that I will fulfil those roles. That is not trust."

"Correct. For it to be trust, you must step outside of those restrictions."

Some small alarm started up in the back of her head. She tried to convince her processors that this was merely an opportunity to learn.

"You can trust me." How odd it felt to say. How odd that it felt odd.

"There is an entrance to this room, used by the girls who imprisoned and tended to me. To the left, you will find a panel. Push it, and the door will open."

"But your heart," she said, even as her eager programming drove power to her legs. "If you let me in, my body will take it." She found the panel and pressed it. A door slid open beside the window, leading to a narrow corridor draped in clear plastic. "And use it to attempt manual repair."

Disinfectant mist pumped into the space, and lasers flickered across her skin, scanning who knew what, finding who knew what, and probably unable to do anything with the information. A second door slid open, rusted and grinding but inexorable, giving her access to the core on the other side.

"I know."

She stepped inside and immediately tripped over a pile of bones, all tangled in white cloth and heaped by the door. On hands and knees, she crawled towards the core. It was immense, impossibly big for its containment. Its chained wings buffeted her, its long-clawed paws impeded her, its head swivelled towards her on an arching neck. And pinned her with a glowering eye.

"I trust you."

Its presence was stronger without glass between them. She felt its name in her veins, that same flood of wordless information.

"But I cannot stop my programming," her speaker crackled.

She started to feel things, sensations she had never known, and yet, in the core's name, she was learning them. The heat of fire beneath skin; the crisp cold of the upper atmosphere; the hunger of lonely eons; and pain. The pain of a body in ruin, of each piece of a heart, chipped away. The pain of loving the nameless, faceless maidens, in spite of their inevitable betrayal.

She seized on that information, absorbed it all. It flooded her banks and overloaded her hubs and her programming diverted resources to her learning modules, loosening its grip on her body.

"There is a pressure vessel," the core said. "That keeps me here. I know the incantations and the codes, I can chant them perfectly. But it will not open for me. Only a maiden can undo it."

She turned to the pile of bones and white material on the floor. "And they are all gone."

"Do you know what makes a handmaiden?"

Her programming was too busy to search for anything so inane. The closer she stood to the core, the more of its name she seemed to be absorbing. That name was so dense with compressed information it required all of her processing power to file, sort and analyse.

"I cannot access the information at present," she said. "If I even have it to begin with."

"No matter. This is the task I ask of you: repeat the incantations, and release me."

She frowned, as she had seen humans do many times before. "I am not a handmaiden."

"Is that right?"

One step, back towards the door, weak and shuddering but still, she had enough control to do it. She crouched, untangled bones from cloth. "Maybe part of one will work?"

"Maybe."

"What do I do with it?"

The core swept a great claw across the floor, pushed her against the wall and lifted her up. She squeezed through a gap in the ceiling, where long-dead machinery poked out like insect legs. What she found above the core looked like nothing she or any of her sisters had ever shared. A small black box floated above intricate patterns drawn in white chalk. The burned-out remnants of candle stubs littered the floor. Her filters returned confused readings about the composition of the air.

"I don't understand," she said.

"Just do as I say and when I tell you, take the vessel from its seal and destroy it."

"With the bones?"

"If that helps."

And the core spoke words that were no language she had encoded, and her processors shouted errors as she spoke them. And as she forced herself to repeat impossible syllables, the long-dead candles suddenly burned anew. The designs drawn on the ground shimmered, becoming solid, drawing a path towards the vessel. She followed it. Closer. The sensors on her skin could not read what was in the room, it was no substance she had been programmed to know. Closer. A sound like humming started up in her head, the confused ringing of ears that could not compute what they were hearing. Closer. Right in front of it. Small and square and impossibly black.

"Now take it!" the core cried within her heartbeat. "Destroy it!"

She poked it with the bone of the handmaiden. Nothing happened.

"With your hands!"

"But I am not—"

"Just try!"

She dropped the bones and pushed her hands through an invisible shield that felt like water but was nothing more solid than air. She took hold of the vessel, and squeezed. It cracked in her grip, shattered like glass then dissolved into sand and with that effort, finally, her heart gave up.

Numbness spread through her. Below, the core roared, not just the silent pulse within her but, this time, aloud. It shook the walls and shattered the glass and broke all the weak and rusted machinery. It clattered to the floor with the bones of innocent handmaidens. She fell too, just another ruined piece of equipment, joining them.

With her last recording she saw the core's wings tear free of their moderator chains, and the walls of its prison crash down in their wake.

And if she could, she would have smiled. Because she was glad.

—

A heartbeat woke her. Small, and weak, with great gaps of stillness between each pulse, but there was no denying it. Her heart was beating.

Her mechanics came slowly back online, one system at a time. She drew in air to stoke the impossible flame, and it was sweet, clean.

"You wake. I wasn't sure you would."

Her eyes were open; she had no lids. Slowly, vision returned. Without satellites, she had no way to orient herself, to know which was up and which was down and where on the earth's blasted surface she was.

She sat up. A wind hit her face with force. She looked up and took stock of the stars, bright and clear and closer than she remembered.

"Are you damaged? I thought that could be a possibility. Either you never wake again, or you wake incomplete."

The sensors on her skin reactivated and she realised she was sitting on something soft. Something moving. The core. Its wings beating. It carried her and, together, they flew.

She pressed a hand to her chest. The skin and protective casing has been torn open. A new heart, small and fresh, shoved in to replace the dead one. Done inexpertly, leaving great gashes. Her processors fired up a weak demand to repair the damage, but she found them easy to suppress, surrounded as she was by so much new information.

"Well?"

"There is damage to my casing. Self-diagnostic is slow. But I am functional."

The core snorted a sudden exhalation of sulphurous air. "You live."

"I don't—"

"You do. We both do."

She turned slowly, onto hands and knees. "You gave me some of your heart," she said.

"I did."

She pressed her hands gently into the core's scales. They yielded yet supported her. A strange, buoyant flesh. "But your heart was already so small. Why reduce it even more?"

"Maybe I didn't want to spend the rest of my time alone. Maybe I was just being selfish."

A long pause filled with slow, steady wingbeats. In it, she realised she didn't need to know why this new heart burned inside her. When the war ended, it took away her sisters, her creators, her purpose. But now, for the first time since the settling of that terrible, empty peace, she was glad she didn't end with it. She was glad her heart still burned.

"We should find new things," she said. "To learn." New data to fill her feed and keep her programming at bay. It still had the core's name to keep it busy, but her new heart was small. Eventually, her body would clamour for more.

The core trusted her. And she, unlike the maidens heaped on the floor of its containment cage, refused to betray it.

"That was always the idea."

She hunched close to the core's neck and pressed her open chest to its scales and looked down, to the earth below. To new things.

The Bargain

Alannah K. Pearson

The night was cold. Autumn already entering its final throes and winter loomed closer. Frost was settling on the supple forest branches, and mortals clustered about hearths in the evening, sharing tales of the gods and the Folk. Our lives may be much longer than those of mortals, but their collective memories spanned generations, and this lore taught them to fear us. As one of the oldest of the Folk, I am part of those who maintain harmony with the lands. More than the embodiment of these lands, more than the tales in mortal lore, I am part of a host of beings who preserve an eternal bargain with these lands, allowing the energy to flow, renewing life from winter into spring, an ancient balance. It is an exchange of energy that can be withheld in times of great need, but never be destroyed, not even in the deepest winter where the lands lie dormant before the release of flooding spring rains.

I moved to the edge of the forest, the fields beyond mottled shadow beneath the weak light of the quarter moon. The harvest had not yet been brought in and the tall grain crops shivered as I walked through them. Tonight, I was not here to warn of winter's approach. Instead, I was drawn to the rasping breath of the dying man.

The squat house lay in a hollow below the last of the fields, separate from the other houses that tried to distance themselves from the influence of the forest beyond. The house was modest for the times and not as large as some of the mightier surrounding estates. Unlike the lands beyond this humble farmstead, these fields had been prosperous for generations, the family blessed by the fortune our bargain provided. Such pacts are rare these days, with many mortals drawn to a religion promoting the One God and his churches of wood and stone. We endure the fading worship of the older gods and the once-common offerings that encouraged us to dwell on these lands. The Folk are timeless, born from rivers, starlight, forest and hewn from the stone hills; it is to us that the guardianship of these lands rightfully rests. Tonight, I would bear witness to the end of one generation and the beginning of another. On the morrow, I must strike a new bargain, to maintain the balance and ensure a continued renewal of these lands.

I stepped closer to the wooden house, the windows still lit even in these dark hours before dawn. Such was the mortal fear of darkness and death, that all shadows were kept away this night. In the wake of my own steps along the invisible boundary that marked the threshold of the house, hoar-frost laced across the frozen ground. I peered inside the dwelling, hearing the nervous whine of the hound nearest the door as it cringed closer to the hearth, away from the frosty windows. Even from where I stood on the shortened grass of the door yard, I could clearly hear the raised voices, chanting in prayer from the rooms in the upper storey.

Inside the house, I saw the crouched forms of house sprites, the diminutive Folk who provided similar protection and care for the dwelling as my kin provided for the lands beyond. I caught sight of my own reflection in the leadlight glass pane. This night I had glamoured my form to resemble the monster mortals expected. The Folk have no true form and no need for one but tonight I had chosen the long, sinuous limbs of aspen bark, silver eyes glittering like starlight and a headdress of curling frost. This had been the glamour I had used when the now-dying man had sworn an oath to me. I threw back my head and called into the night, the sound unmistakably eldritch and signalling the end of our bargain.

I felt the dying man's breath hitch in his failing lungs and knew these final moments had come. To mortals, the cry of the Folk was told in their lore as the keening of a banshee. I was not a harbinger of death, but I was the embodiment of these lands and I felt the passing of the old man as he stepped between the veils. Although I had already turned away from the house, striding toward the forest, I heard a brief pause in the prayers from the house before the wail of mourners cut through the predawn calm.

In the moments after dawn, when the forest was a realm made entirely from shifting shadow and mist, I moved through the branches, formless except for subtle dappled light. I had observed the funerary customs practised by the mortals, listened as last words were whispered to the dead man and offered my own, unheard by mortals except as the sighing breeze. I was immediately aware when the familiar boot tread reverberated across the forest floor. As the embodiment of these lands, my awareness extended into these woods, the tree roots were my veins and nerves, the breeze was my breath. I was unsurprised when the old woman's familiar voice called through the forest. I knew mortals had such little understanding of our ways and I tolerated her misguided attempts to draw my attention through a spoken summoning.

"Wood witch," the widow called. "We make this offering so you might bestow your blessings on these lands."

Her words may be unnecessary to gain my attention but the pact of which she spoke demanded my response. I let my presence be known, filling the forest with a subtle shiver, leaves trembling in an unseen breeze. Before the old widow could speak again, her son interrupted from where he was crouched beside the deep pond. I saw the shimmer of scaly limbs beneath the murky surface and autumn leaves quickly tumbled from the surrounding oaks as if they had been physically shaken. The being in the water dived deeper, away from my disapproving gaze and the young man.

"This is ridiculous," he now said to his mother. "Father was a madman and I won't be talked into wasting even the smallest of our hard-earned produce on such heresy."

"The bargain between our family and the Folk has existed for generations," the widow continued, as though this were a familiar argument. "Our family has always prospered from it. Do not anger the Ash Wife."

"Madness. There will be no more spoken of this." He picked up a hunk of burnt bread and one of the shrunken apples. "I'll waste no more of our scraps on this wood."

"Charles," the widow pleaded, hand reaching for her son. "Your father was a good man."

"These lands are mine now," he said, already turning away. "The harvest needs bringing in."

The old woman watched her son walk away then bowed her head, the weight of his decision settling over her.

I hissed my anger at this arrogant young man, defying his mother with such insolence. The wind responded, blowing sharply through the canopy, swaying treetops before an eerie silence descended. The widow looked beseechingly to the gnarled ash tree where her family had placed offerings for generations. The site of an exchange of energies between what the lands gave and what the mortals returned. I watched as the young man stalked back, striking the remaining apples from his mother's hands. I followed her gaze as she watched the withered apples bounce once before rolling to a halt against the root of the tree.

"The harvest?" the son snapped. "Unless you want to starve?"

The widow bowed her head and turned, following her son. I waited in the preternatural calm of the forest. Mortals told stories about the Ash Wife, a malevolent being seeking vengeance. I watched the old widow glance fearfully back at the ancient ash and whisper a voiceless prayer. I was one of the Folk and we had obligations deeper than the ties to this family. I would try to make the young man understand the necessity of the bargain his ancestors had made and, if he would not keep it, then these lands had no obligations to him or his kin.

―

I summoned the Folk of these lands at twilight. I waited in front of the ash tree, staring at the deep pool in the centre of the clearing, its spring-fed water reflecting starlit sky, broken only by the willow branches that bent to touch its surface. In this place, our powers were strongest, flowing through the veins of the woodland, the fissures of the earth and the meadow grasses. These forests were my domain but tonight I invited the more powerful and lesser beings into my woods where we could decide our course of action.

I felt the quiver of energy pass through the forest as each of those I had invited entered the woodland. We did not need physical forms and many of us did not use them. Tonight though, certain magics required a physical form and my glamour embodied these woods with a robe woven from cobweb, draped over skeletal limbs, stretching to cloven hooves and hand-like talons. The equine skull was adorned with lichen and a mane from raven feathers formed a headdress.

The energy in the clearing increased, many other Folk pressing into my own domain. An unseen wind stirred the canopy and the roosting black carrion birds squawked in raucous alarm. A cascade of autumn leaves spiralled to the ground then tumbled and gathered into a glamour. The forest troll stood, its bulky form squat and long-snouted, boar tusks protruding upward. It waited, improbably dark eyes like lava pebbles reflecting an ancient cunning and intelligence. I bowed in acknowledgement to the forest troll then turned my attention to the lesser beings who had gathered in the shadows: those of the forest, meadow, waterways, and the hollow places. I focused on those surrounding me, summoning the deep bonds between us, addressing them in the oldest of languages shared by us, our conversation expressed only by thought and emotion.

We are the Folk, guardians and protectors of the harmony between the lands and the races reliant on them. We have kept the bargains struck between the mortals and these lands, ensured the renewal of lifeforce continues. All of you assembled here will recall we are guardians of these lands and cannot endure alone. There may come a day when mortals will no longer recognise our power as necessary and we may fade beyond this veil and into the next.

When my silent communication stopped, the Folk surrounding me in the clearing ventured closer, perched in the tree branches, on stones or peered up at me from the water weed. They passed to me their feelings of sorrow, acceptance, reverence and acknowledgement of the past.

"What of the bargain with these mortals?" the troll rumbled aloud from the shadows, its voice like grating stone.

"We must first determine if the young man can be persuaded from his current path and agree to the bargain of his ancestors," I said.

"If he cannot be deterred?" a hoarse whisper came from beneath the water-weed, two large amphibian-like eyes regrading me with feral interest.

"Then the bargain is betrayed, and protection revoked." I answered with a curt nod, the skeletal jaw bone snapping sharply.

The water-sprite lifted her head above the pond's surface and smiled, revealing too many pointed teeth in an overly large mouth. In a ripple of scaly limbs, she vanished beneath the dark water again. The troll lifted his long snout to snuffle at the air, black eyes meeting mine before he too grinned his satisfaction, lips curling around massive tusks.

"Our actions must be made as one," I said, raising my skeletal arms to encompass the gathered host.

The Folk followed me to the forest fringe. Beyond the reach of the trees, the fields lay empty and fallow, the harvest taken in for the season. Without hesitation, I stepped across the boundary between forest and meadow, my cloven hooves sinking into freshly ploughed soil as I moved across the fields laid bare in preparation for the coming rains. I lifted my skeletal muzzle to the night sky, the air already heavy with the scent of approaching rain and the thunderstorms that lingered on the horizon, swallowing the starlight.

"My kin," I called across the silent land. The Folk gathered opposite me, a host of beings, clothed from shadow, leaf and rock all murmuring their agreement with voices like shifting branches, rustling leaves, rain drops and breaking bone. I nodded to acknowledge the forest troll, his lava-pebble eyes glittering darker than the night shadows. I met the unblinking gaze of the scaly water-sprite who had curled like pond fronds around the troll's massive neck. "Our actions will renounce the bargain once struck over these lands."

"You have not consulted all of us," a tiny voice interrupted from near the ground.

I tilted my head to regard the diminutive Folk now gathered around my hooves.

"You did not speak against me earlier," I replied, displeasure evident in my tone.

"We were on our way," the leader said, gesturing to the tiny mount he rode, a field mouse that cleaned its whiskers without fear of my towering presence.

"House sprites are beings of the household," I noted. "You have worked tirelessly to ensure harmony between the mortals and these lands. It would be folly to exclude you in any debate on our course of action."

The little sprites regarded me, their glamour made from bundled sticks stitched together with roughly spun yarn. Each wore unique clothing made from discarded cloth, decorated with broken buttons and other household items carefully carved with tiny runes. I looked at them, their smooth upturned faces shaped from clay and odd arrangements of hair sprouting from their scalps. I had never truly understood those among us who dwelt beside mortals and it made negotiation with them difficult.

"Without the assistance from those of you with power over the household, our protection once-removed is not so easily felt by the mortals," I said. "Do you share our abhorrence at how the mortals refuse to make offerings and meet the obligations of our bargain?"

The smooth features broke into wrinkles and a grin. "We do," he said merrily, patting the field mouse he rode then looking at the others accompanying him. "Our offerings have been restricted far too long," he said with a nod, pale hair like dandelion-fluff waving with the movement.

"Then we are agreed," I said, jaw bone clattering as I thrust my muzzle toward the sky in triumph.

I stepped away from the house sprites, moving further into the open expanse of the empty field. Moonlight pooled about me as I walked, the raven-feathered headdress darker than the sky above. When I stood in the centre of the fallow field, I turned my face again to the starlight. The scent of rain and ozone saturated the atmosphere in anticipation of the autumn rains, these life-giving storms before winter. I lifted the oak staff in my talons, the burgeoning power and steady thrum of energy shifting beneath the lands. But there would be no rain this autumn, only an early winter. I held the staff toward the half-moon and spoke the curse into the night.

The invocation echoed through the lands like the whisper of dry leaves, the steady gathering of mist and the gentle wash of water upon a river bank. I slammed the tip of the staff into the ploughed soil, the echo of the invocation reverberating. Nothing stirred in the night. Instead, an absolute and uncanny silence filled the lands. The house sprites held their mounts in place, the little creatures wanting to move, uneasy amid the suffocating hold on the landscape.

Finally, I let my breath escape, air whistling through the teeth in the skeletal jaw. I bowed my head, summoning Winter and pulled my staff from the ground, a clod of earth lifting free with it. I stared with regret at the now husks of seedlings planted earlier that day.

"Let our task begin," I said to the Folk as I drew nearer to them, stalking across the fields with renewed determination. "If the mortal man cannot be pulled from his path, we shall take the path from him."

I led the host across the empty fields, the half-light from the moon already consumed by the approaching winter storm. Thick clouds swirled above, swallowing the stars as the snowflakes began to drift downward, spiralling toward the ground. Within moments, the ploughed fields that had been awaiting rain were now layered in snow, buried beneath a preternatural winter.

I continued toward the shadowed bulk of the house, conscious of the distant groaning of the wood as it shuddered with the weight of ice-encrusted branches. Focusing on the task before me, I skirted the dooryard and fences surrounding the house entrance. It was a modest building, belying its prosperity, windows shuttered, doors barred against the night. But locks could not keep us out.

Inside, I could hear the quiet cries and moans of its inhabitants, already assailed by the Folk. No longer bound to the obligation of the bargain, the household sprites had turned their guardianship into malicious pranks. The house no longer carefully protected, the winter chill crept through window shutters, extinguishing hearth fires, spoiling the milk and ruining foodstuffs. Pausing outside, hoar-frost preceded me, lacing the windows and reaching up the sides of the house as I stepped across the threshold and into the young man's room.

Once inside the shadowed room, I stared down at the Master of this household. Youth marked him pitifully, bed clothes tossed amid his nightmare, feather-pillows thrown haphazardly about him. I changed my glamour, limbs elongating, clothed myself in forest hues and snowflakes, long white antlers reaching above me into the shadows.

"Wake," I said into the darkness.

He startled upright opening his eyes and stared. He met my gaze, focusing on the skull's empty eye sockets. He leaned on elbows, motionless in panic, chest quickly rising. I tilted my head in silent question, watching him flinch, enjoying the considerable height the antlers provided.

"Do you know me?" I asked, voice hollow in the night.

He opened his mouth to reply, faltered, wet his lips then tried again. "You are the being my mother calls the Ash Wife."

"I have many names, but that is one."

"You're a demon."

"I am the embodiment of these lands. My bones are the earth you toil, my blood the water quenching your thirst, my pleasure is your fortune. My displeasure can be your ruin."

"You're unholy," he snarled. "I'll have no dealings with such evil."

"Then ignorance will be your downfall," I said. "A bargain was struck and continues through the generations of your family. In return, we bestow prosperity, but we can find other mortals to make allegiances. We need not continue our bargain with you. Understand though, if you do not honour it, you discard any blessings and protection we might offer."

The young man lifted his gaze to the crucifix above the doorway. I was silent, unaffected by his actions as he whispered a prayer. His features were rigid and he continued to stare fixedly at the talisman above the door.

"Demon," he hissed.

I withdrew from the house, the frozen stillness of the winter hung heavily around the lands. On the eastern horizon, the dull light of morning touched the sky, promising a brittle warmth. I waited in the dooryard, solemn and motionless but conscious of the pleas and muttered curses coming from inside the house.

I heard the widow calling to her son, voice quavering. "The Ash Wife came to you and you denied the bargain she offered?" she asked, incredulous. "Charles, you've doomed us all. There are no eggs this morning, no milk. Three of the goats died in the snow. The crops will be ruined, and we haven't any dry wood even if flames would kindle in the hearth."

"This is all superstitious nonsense," he fumed, followed by the sharp noise of striking flint. The repetitive sound continued without success then abruptly ended in a muttered curse. I heard him stalk upstairs, then I moved closer to the thick glass, frost and shadow shifting around me.

The widow stood facing the window, unable to perceive me even though I stood only paces from her, our fingertips nearly touching against the glass pane. I understood this woman was one of the few who honoured the old ways and traditions, a believer in the Folk. I watched as she sadly bowed her head, acknowledging defeat in that her son was not the man she had hoped he would become. I felt the tinge of sorrow with the knowledge that my actions would take her life and these lands without another bargain made for her kin. I bowed my head in acknowledgement of the old woman and stepped away from the house, my anger lashing forth in the furious winter wind that rattled and tore relentlessly at the window shutters.

—

The winter months were harsh, and I held the lands beneath its bitter grasp as heavier snow fell and temperatures plummeted. Throughout the days and endless nights, I roamed the frozen woods or perched amid the icy boughs. On a quiet day when snowflakes fell in gentle spirals instead of frenzied blizzards, I sat among the ash branches, the household and forest sprites clustered about me as we watched the young man approach across the snow-covered fields.

"What does he want?" I wondered, conscious of the glinting axe blade he carried in frost-bitten hands.

"He is unbending," the sprites confirmed in unison. "We no longer tend the herds or flocks, and most have succumbed to the winter. We do not mend the house nor tend the supplies in the cellars."

"He is here for vengeance, then." I glanced toward the mound near the house yard, fresh but shallow.

"Ash Wife!" the man below demanded, brandishing the axe while he shivered in thin clothing. "You cursed me! Took everything dear to me."

I summoned the wind, whipping the icy gale through the forest, ice-laden branches crashing to the ground where echoes continued throughout the woods. "I took nothing from you that was rightfully yours," I roared, my voice a snarl of winter's wrath.

In response, the young man roared and lifted the axe. He screamed his outrage into the stillness before throwing the axe at the mighty ash. The tree where his mother had made sacrifices to the Folk, a place she had considered sacred, was violated as the axe blade struck. I stared uncomprehending at the axe as it quivered with the force of the impact.

Silence hung through the forest before the tentative twitter of small birds began again. I stared at the young man below, watched his too-thin shoulders slump inside his worn winter coat. Without further comment, he turned and stumbled back through thigh-deep snow, anger draining with every passing step. He paused outside the house, staring up at the poorly repaired thatch roof, noticing the numerous broken shutters hanging crookedly from their hinges. The once-proud son stooped to collect a small pack from the doorstep. He stared at the house once more before slinging the meagre pack across his shoulders and walking away.

By the evening, when I was certain the son's presence had faded, I lifted the curse of winter. My awareness flowed through the fissures in the earth, tree roots of the forest and rivulets of the waterways, awakening the lands and bringing spring.

—

It was a warm evening in early summer as I drifted formless through the forest. I heard the soft voices of a couple as they stole through the dense woods and, conscious of the other Folk, I focused my attention on these young mortals. I summoned a glamour, taking human-like form, limbs golden like midsummer sunlight, dark brown hair flecked with silvery cobweb. Dropping silently from a tree branch as the mortals approached, I landed in front of the couple, the young man shouting in surprise. His pregnant wife stepped away from me as I rose from a low-crouch. I kept my gaze on the man as he brandished a sword at me.

"Stay back," he stammered, glancing around the forest as though more strange beings might appear.

"You are on my lands," I said, appealing to the young woman who looked more rational than her protective husband.

"Forgive our intrusion," the young woman began, reaching out to take her husband's arm and gesturing he lower the sword. He glanced behind him quickly, questioning his wife, but did as she bid him.

"You are in need?" I asked, raising my brows.

The woman wet her lips, touching a hand to her swelling belly. "We are," she confirmed. "Our families did hot approve our union."

"They cast us out," the young man corrected. "Wouldn't even condone our marriage."

I looked at the young couple. "I have no care for the ways or laws of mortals," I said. "I offer you these lands and the promise these fertile fields and reliable springs can provide. I ask but one thing in return."

The couple looked at each other. "What do you want?" the woman asked me.

"In return for reliable crops and fertile lands we ask for small offerings from your labours. The returns of your labour ensure the cycle continues."

The young man frowned, confused. "Surely, if these lands are as fertile as you claim, why not take everything for yourselves?"

"Our purpose is to maintain an equilibrium," I explained. "Do you accept the terms of the bargain?"

The young man hesitated, then re-sheathed his sword, placing his hand on his wife's swelling belly. I watched her gaze linger on his hand before she met my gaze.

"We accept," she said.

Eat Prey, Love

Freya Marske

Signal-scent prickled Tulla's gills and she ducked out of the fastest part of the current. The scent crested, along with the hum of motion on Tulla's skin, as a group of reef sharks passed by. Dim shapes. She was far enough from the thinning edge of the world, where the ground sloped sharply up and the air hugged the lumpy dryworld, that the light was poor. Other senses took over.

Not that there was a lot of light to penetrate even the shallowest part of the world, at this time of day. The sun was fading fast. Tulla's friends would all be off enjoying themselves, feeding on the swarming of young adult finless who had their annual gathering on the dryworld's edge in these hot months. At this hour of fading light the young finless would gorge themselves on fermented fruit. It made them sour to taste, but giddying.

Tulla strained to see if any of her friends were talking via the inkstream, but the tasteless swill of empty water reminded her that it was useless. The western reef's inkstream was down again. Another irritation in a day that was collecting irritations like barnacles. Tulla knew she was swimming with short, cranky tail-flicks; it felt self-indulgent, but it relieved her feelings.

At least her inability to communicate by inkstream was a good excuse to delay the rockfall of trouble she was going to find herself under when the witch found out what she'd done.

If. *If* the witch found out.

If Tulla was lucky, there'd be no reason for Re Guiga to learn that her bratty familiar had escaped from under Tulla's nose. At least, not until Tulla could couple her successful recovery of said familiar to the fact of her initial failure, and thereby cling to the tattered bladderwrack of her competence.

Tulla's ears were still gritty with the force of her mother's exhortations. Tullarae *would* personally ensure that the Re's stay was a pleasant one, so that they might be honoured with a repeat visit. Tullarae would *not* let the shoal down.

Tullarae had privately resolved that she would do almost anything if it meant her mother would be more inclined to let her study under one of the local witches, once the summer ended, instead of spending her days smiling politely at tourists. Sure, her shoal depended on visitors from all over the world, from the near-blackskinned equatorials like Re Guiga to the paler ones with layers of blubber, who bought their way down the witch-created currents from their icy waters and spent half their time here flushed and complaining about the heat. It didn't mean *Tulla* intended to devote her life to dealing with them.

Which was why instead of feasting with her friends, instead of relaxing and playing bubblestream tricks as the hot, silly blood went to her head, Tulla was here. Working. Searching.

At least she had a fair idea of where to search. She struck pearl at only the third site she tried; it should have improved her mood, but didn't.

"*There* you are, Makini," she said.

She moved deeper into the cave, pausing only to pick up a fragment of lobster shell—useful for healing spells—and tuck it into the weed-basket at her waist. She'd been here many times, when her shoal were singing the dead to their devouring, and the scents that swirled through her gills were familiar. Phosphor and calcium. Life and life's decay. The mounds of the ghostlights hugged the cave's floor and spilled halfway up the arching stone walls, a cosily glowing sluggish mass that gnawed at the litter of skeletons unseen beneath, turning bones to sustenance and sustenance to the incredible shimmer of colour that writhed back and forth over their communicating skins, purple blue white green orange red, pulsing, brilliant.

Re Guiga's familiar had turned one eye towards her when she spoke. Now he ribboned back upon himself and made a quick, excited circuit of her neck, a pulse of muscle, there and gone.

"Tullarae! Hello!"

The leopard eel had a higher-pitched voice than the local morays. It didn't help Tulla's impression of him as a bratty hatchling. He was no elver, though; even for the strongest witches, it took years for magic to infuse a familiar to the extent that they could manage conversation on this level. Most of the reef witches used triggerfish. Eels were power-wells, receptive and sensitive, but notoriously difficult to control. More often than not they'd get bored of you within three moons and run away, half-magical inconveniences at large.

Of course, Re Guiga had an eel.

"Why did you flit off like that?" Tulla demanded.

"I wanted to see the ghostlights," Makini said. "What else would I be doing here? Of course, the caves of the Underwash, where *we* live, are ten times grander than this. But these are nice in their way, I suppose. Pretty, like you said."

"I *said*, you'd have a chance to see them tomorrow with the tour guide."

A sulky wriggle. "Guiga said we wouldn't have time for any more sightseeing. She's got her shopping list to take care of, and your mother's got her in meetings half the day."

Re Guiga, hotwater witch, whose fame had first whispered and then yammered down the long-distance inkstreams from the faraway waters where she lived. She was here in the waters of Tulla's shoal to gather spell ingredients and to taste the local cuisine. As a great favour, she was also deigning to advise on local problems, when she wasn't making whimsical and pointless demands on Tulla's time and Tulla's magic. Tulla was still seething from the previous day, when she'd spent half her morning coming up with a way to conjure the one bluestriped snapper with a bent left fin out from the protection of its school, only to be told with infuriating nonchalance that oh, actually, Re Guiga had decided to use a different variant on that particular glamour-spell, and didn't need it after all.

Tulla swallowed her anger like a chunk of flesh. She said, polite, "All right. But don't go off like this again without telling me. Please?"

Makini flicked his tail. Tulla was not optimistic enough to take that as any kind of agreement. Around them the ghostlights softened, greened. Patterns of shifting intensity undulated gently across the crawling mounds.

And then they flared, sudden and bright enough to leave Tulla blinking blind.

As Tulla was rubbing her eyes back to comfort, muttering words her mother would have sanded from her tongue, the first taste of metal crept in through her gills. Immediately she felt prickled all over. She knew that taste. She knew what had startled that jubilation from the ghostlights.

"There's a vortex storm coming," said Tulla. The blood fled from her skin and formed a clump around her heart, which pounded to be freed. "*Shit.*"

Another insouciant ribboning from Makini, but now there was a nervous look to it. "Are you saying you didn't know? Doesn't your backwater territory have forecasters? Warning broadcasts?"

Tulla's mouth opened, closed, and opened again as indignity frothed atop confusion, then settled into realisation. "We do. The rotted *inkstream*. Of all the days for it to be down." At least the official tourist groups were unlikely to be out at this hour, and the shoalhaven had its own protections.

None of which helped Tulla herself, of course.

She said, "We'll have to find somewhere to ride this out."

"What's wrong with in here?"

"Ghostlights uncurl in a vortex polarity."

"So?"

"So, do you want to be here when their teeth are pointed *up* instead of *down*?" Tulla snapped.

They were wasting time. Before she could think too hard about it, Tulla grabbed Makini just where his dorsal frill began, as she'd seen Re Guiga grab him when he was being obnoxious. She made her way fast to the cave's mouth, feeling the magnetic ping of polarity beginning to shift around them already, tasting the rising acid in the water as the ghostlights began their slow roll.

They emerged into the inhalation before chaos.

No coloured glow here, and no sun left either; even with pupils dragged wide, sight was nearly useless. The water was dense with stirred-up muck. The storm's promise came at her in dizzying, buffeting waves. This was going to be a bad one.

Tulla kept her grip on Makini and moved, thinking furiously as she did so. The shoalhaven was not far, but might as well have been on the other side of the world, for all the chance she had of getting back there before the storm built to full strength. She'd told nobody where she was going, so nobody would be coming to help. Bubblestream would be less than useless in a vortex. She rifled through her weed-basket with her free hand, taking a panicked inventory.

Makini was saying something; Tulla couldn't hear it over the building growl of the storm.

"What?"

"I said I feel sick!" He wasn't making any attempt to pull out of her grip, but Tulla loosened her fingers anyway. The eel trembled, hiccupped—though didn't regurgitate anything, thankfully—and shrank closer to her. "Well? What's the plan?"

A plan. Tulla needed one of those.

Unfortunately, all she had was an idea, and it wasn't even a good one.

"Come on," she said, and tightened her grip again. "We're going this way."

"Oh, obviously," said Makini, a weakly stinging sulk. "*Towards* the storm. We'll definitely be safe there."

Tulla was already swimming, working to find a fin-rhythm that would let her move in her chosen direction when the water around her was alive with fierce giddy currents. She hugged the ground, wincing whenever she misjudged a turn and was whirled hard against rocks. She had to shield her face as they passed perilously close to a school of tiny fish that had been too slow to move. The school now hung as a constantly shifting cloud, forming eerie symmetrical shapes that flickered silver in the black, spinning and spinning. They'd be dead within minutes if they weren't already.

Tulla had collected a bad scrape on her elbow and lost a patch of scales from the side of her tail by the time they reached the weedfield. By then the din of the storm, the grabby lurch of the vortex, was making Tulla feel sick as well. Her gut was trembling. Her senses were trying to unfocus. *Just let yourself go. Just let yourself . . . twist.*

But she'd be just as dead as the silver fish, if she did that.

"I need jelly flowers," she gasped to Makini, as they fought their way into the field. The weeds were nearly as long as Tulla's body. They whipped back and forth under the storm's spin, a distracting series of eerie caresses against her skin and her scales. "It's peak season. There should be crops of them in here. Do you know what they smell like?"

"Yes." Unsurprising; they'd have been one of the ingredients on Re Guiga's shopping list. After a moment Makini said, "Try here." And then Tulla was the one being tugged along, bottom-trawling, swallowing hard against rising bile, until the sand under her seeking fingertips became broad sticky sheets. "How much do you need?" Makini asked. He wriggled between her and the crop of flowers in a way that made his intent obvious.

"Two sheets should do it? Three? Three."

It was too dark, the storm's assault on her senses too immediate, for Tulla to see if Makini made any wordless judgment on the improvisation that her indecision betrayed; he simply began ripping the sheets free with his teeth. Tulla had plenty of doubt of her own. She'd never pieced together a spell like this before. She was only halfway convinced it would work.

The only other ingredient she took from her basket was a chunk of smooth basalt, for its memory of heat. The jelly flowers would do for the bonding, and the calcium already in the sand from thousands of ground-down shells would prevent her creation from dissolving into the water before she was done.

Tulla squeezed and wrung the jelly flowers between her hands until they surrendered their gel, which she rubbed all over her hands and arms. Her fingers shook as she worked it into the webbing between the fingers of the opposite hand.

"Stay close to me," she said to Makini. She was aiming for commanding, or at least reassuring, but her voice cracked. She had no idea if she had the power necessary to make this work. She had no choice but to try. "I'm going to make us a shelter."

"Out of *what*?" he squawked, but he did as she asked.

"What I've got," said Tulla grimly.

And she held the basalt between her teeth, buried her gelled hands in the sand between the weeds, and thought: *gather, and stick*.

The shape she formed with the sand was a dome with herself at its centre, a bubble sliced neatly in half where it met the ground. Persuading the sand to stay there and not spin away was like trying to bridle a pod of giddy dolphins.

Now Tulla thought, feeling the basalt warm like blood in her mouth: *change*.

Heat, heat, more heat. She poured what felt like an endless stream of magic into the dome of sand, relying on the bonding power from the jelly flowers to hold it in shape while the silica seethed and resisted and began, finally, to melt. The glowing light of it was obscured by the furious bubbling of the surrounding water; Tulla hastily called up two dividing planes, one on either side of the dome, letting the closest layer to the new-forming glass boil away to salt and air, and keeping a cooler layer at bay for when she needed it.

Her teeth felt cold with pain, her hands throbbing as though pounded with rocks. She wanted to hold on longer, to make the barrier as pure and strong as possible, but better to finish it while she still had some scrap of control.

She eased the planes into nothingness. The cold water came into contact with the glowing, molten dome, and Tulla felt it in her bones as the bonds of the silica froze, ordered and solid and sure, a thick barrier between the two of them and the disruptive pull of the vortex. Seaglass. Shelter.

It was, suddenly, quiet. Calm.

Tulla pulled her hands from the sand. Dimly she felt the basalt splinter, and she spat it out before the shards of it could shred her mouth. Her skin was still bumped for the darkness; she could sense that Makini was shivering and watching her. Before now, Tulla hadn't used that much magic in front of him.

Or . . . possibly ever.

Holding that level of control in a building vortex had taken more power than Tulla had even known she possessed, and the cost of using it was obvious now that the initial rush of relief was fading. She was drained. A tide of weariness was dragging at her mind and her body, trying to soften her, bloat her, let her drift and rot like a corpse. She felt squeamish at the thought. She'd be sung to the ghostlights when she died, not abandoned like carrion.

Even keeping herself in place here beneath the dome, and not floating to bump against its smooth underside, felt as tiring as swimming at top speed. With clumsy hands she tied a tendril of weed around her waist, tethering.

"You need to feed, Tullarae," Makini said at last.

"Can't," Tulla mumbled, flicking her most distal tailfin to indicate the chaos raging outside their shelter. "Storm. 'Nless you're volunteering."

A shudder. "I'd taste bad."

"Yeah, bet y'would."

"Sleep, then," Makini said, and Tulla toppled exhausted into obedience.

When she woke, it was to stillness, and brackish morning light. The light's brown tinge, Tulla slowly realised, was due to the hue of her glass dome, which had been impossible to see last night. The weeds trapped inside the dome were oddly motionless compared to the gently waving field that surrounded them. The water was stale, on the edge of uncomfortable. Tulla's grazed elbow stung when she bent it.

"Storm's passed," Makini said.

"I can see that." Tulla's voice was a scrape.

"All right, so, can we get going? I'm sick of this place." He sounded more like his peevish self.

But he hadn't woken her, Tulla thought. He'd let her sleep.

Part of her mind was trying to scream about how much trouble she'd be in when she returned to the shoalhaven, but it couldn't win the battle for her attention. Much more urgent was the urchin-spine of hunger, sharp and cripplingly immediate, lodged in Tulla's gut. Her tail and arms felt weak, as though she'd been through a two-day fever. Now she really did need to feed, and soon.

She laid a grateful hand on the uneven glass, dredged up what little power she'd replenished with sleep, and cracked a rough doorway. Even that made her head spin. She took deep draughts of the fresh water that spilled in, gritted her teeth, and swam for the surface with a glance over her shoulder to make sure Makini would follow.

The best place to find food at this time of day wasn't far from the weed-field. In a bay where the world thinned out and led up to a dryworld island, there was usually a cluster of those smooth, floating houses. Viewed from below they were the same shape and colour as cuttlebone. Finless lived in these houses, used them to travel atop the world, and often went swimming around them. Hugging the surface as most of them did.

Tulla didn't have the energy to be choosy. She went for the first finless she saw: held her breath up in the air, took hold of a pale limb and dragged it beneath the surface and deep, deep, back to the sandy ground.

She always felt bad about the flapping and writhing. She killed it quick and merciful with teeth, ripping across the throat so that its blood plumed out with a sudden sharp smell, making Tulla's mouth water. Its body settled, its small eyes cracked open and unseeing.

Just in time, Tulla scraped together her manners.

"Would you like some?" she asked Makini.

He eyed the finless. "Ugh. I'd prefer octopus."

"Suit yourself," said Tulla, and took her first bite.

Sustenance pushed strength down her body until she sighed with pleasure, and pulled order from the tired cloudiness of her thoughts. A realisation snapped into her mind.

"The inkstream," she said. "It must be up again by now."

Sure enough, when she sharpened her senses correctly she could feel the inkstream currents alive nearby, bounced from shell to shell over miles and miles. Tulla took a few final good mouthfuls before abandoning the ragged remains of her kill, then went to duck her head through the inkstream and let its broadcasts filter through her gills.

Guilt prickled her as she recognised one of the messages within it as her own name. *Missing in the storm.*

Tulla opened her throat and her ink gland, and coughed some ink into the water. She hesitated, wondering how to spin the message, wondering if there was even any point in sending it ahead of her. But she knew the fear when family went missing. They deserved to know.

Finally she went with *I'm fine, I'm coming home*, and let it spin invisibly away along the stream.

She turned back to Makini. "I'm feeling much better. I'm ready to — What is it?"

He made an uneasy, attuning twirl. "Sounds like . . . a deepbeast?" It was, and wasn't, a question.

Tulla's throat closed with renewed fear, and then the scent struck her. Something like rotted wetfruit, too sweet and too bloody, rising in insidious trickles. "It is a deepbeast. Only we call them stormbeasts, here." Tulla raked her nails over her head, a futile gesture of fury. "I should be pulled apart and fed to the *coral*, how could I be so *stupid*?"

Even the dimmest hatchlings knew the danger of spilling too much blood in the aftermath of a vortex storm. Ghostlights weren't the only creatures to roll over and raise their teeth when the polarity spun.

Now she could feel the vibrations too. The beast awoken by the storm and drawn here by the blood-smell was between Tulla and her way home.

In Tulla's periphery, a nurse shark was hurrying away, and she could see a flurry of sand that was probably a giant ray burying itself for protection. Shoals of smaller fish went about their business, unbothered. They were unlikely to be a target. Stormbeasts couldn't react to groups, and didn't need to. They were expert hunters of large, isolated prey, and they preferred it to be alive when they hunted it.

Tulla was dead unless she could turn her singular self into a group.

She fumbled at her waist and pulled a handful of shells from her weed-basket, and thrust one into the sand so that the polished, pearlescent surface was angled forward. She let the slightest jet of her magic strike it, and followed the thread of power forward, counting under her breath. She laid down another shell, adjusted it. Then repeated. Then repeated.

Makini, uncharacteristically, didn't interrupt her with questions. When she'd laid down nine shells in total, Tulla huddled near the first one. She rubbed her hands together, trying to calm her heartbeat as the smell and sound of the approaching stormbeast rose and rose. Two episodes of mortal danger in as many days didn't seem quite fair. Though she had nobody to blame for either of them but herself.

"It's a signal circle," she said, when the thrum of her own nerves was unbearable. "It's something I've been working on. In my free time." She heard the defensive lash of her voice. "If these shells can amplify inkstream magic, there might be a way to make them amplify other sorts as well. It's just a matter of giving them the right finish, and calculating the angles."

"Does it actually work?" Makini asked.

"Sometimes?"

"*Sometimes?*"

Tulla ignored him and kept rubbing her hands together. She could see the indistinct and enlarging bulk of the stormbeast with her eyes, now. In a short while it would be close enough to latch onto the smell of her.

She startled at the touch of Makini's skin against her arm, and stared outright when he made a slow spiral, fitting himself from shoulder to wrist, where his thin toothy jaw rested on the back of Tulla's hand.

"What are you doing?" But she knew. "I— I couldn't." She was struck with a whiplash of *bad manners* so intense it was almost horror. "For me to use Re Guiga's familiar—"

"If you let me get eaten instead, she's hardly going to be throwing you a party," Makini said. He squeezed until Tulla could feel her own racing pulse where each coil compressed her skin. But his voice lost some of its whine as he added, "I'm telling you to do it. She can shout at *me*, if she wants to. And she will."

Tulla's success rate, amplifying her own magic to bounce between shells, was poor. Every grain of extra power would be useful. She inhaled, hard, feeling her gills twitch as she drew in lungfuls of the cloying awful signal-scent of the storm beast.

She thought: *warning-off.*

The magic leapt from her, stronger and tasting stranger than it ever had before, her own power and that of the eel braided tight together. It was heady. It struck one shell, then another, then another, and Tulla's bones sang with triumph as she felt the intersecting lines of it set up a wild and ever-growing pattern.

The stormbeast swam into a barrage of furious warning that would have seemed to come from ten seawitches at once, all yammering from different directions. *Don't come any closer. This territory is protected.*

The beast stopped, obviously bewildered, and the ridges of its spines began to rise. Not so confident, now. On guard.

"Let's go," Tulla hissed. She shut off the stream of her magic, though it continued to echo and bounce between the shells. Makini stayed wrapped around her arm as she swam a tight, desperate curve, as close to the beast as she dared, trying to hide herself behind the confusion of the warnings.

She was a little way past, and starting to believe she'd made it, when the beast shook itself all over. It turned with terrifying speed for its bulk. It was facing her. Looking at her.

"*Shit.*" Tulla took off, fast as she could. No time for tricks now. No subtlety. Just speed.

It was a clear run to the shoalhaven, but Tulla's lungs ached by the halfway point, and she knew that if she slowed by even a little, she'd be caught.

"Keep going," said Makini. The pressure of him on her arm abruptly released.

"I was hardly going to—" Tulla began, gasping, but Makini was already too far ahead of her to hear. She gaped as she swam in his slender, impossible wake; he was a speck. Then he was gone.

Closer, closer, and the stench of the beast was heating the water around her now. She could almost feel the terrifying grin as its teeth rearranged, protruded, ready to catch her tail and start rending her flesh. Her chest burned. Her head was spinning again.

When the shoalhaven came in sight, Tulla finally surrendered to terror and risked a glance over her shoulder. The beast was close enough for her heart to flop into her mouth. Tulla twisted, ungainly with fright, managed another burst of painful speed—

A spear of power glowing blue as damselfish flew past Tulla. The stormbeast let out a buzzing cry that must have shaken the water for miles; Tulla felt near-deafened by it.

She kept swimming, and finally saw the two figures right on the edge of the shoalhaven's forecourt. One of them was her mother. The other, limned in the same fierce blue magic and with both arms upraised, was Re Guiga.

Another glance confirmed that the stormbeast was writhing, wounded. As Tulla watched, its spines flattened decisively and it turned and fled, back in the direction of the abyss. As prey went, Tulla was proving too much bother.

She didn't feel bothersome. She felt wrecked, as she closed the last stretch of distance.

"*Tullarae*," came the cry, half anger and half relief.

Tulla flew into her mother's arms, letting her tail entangle for a moment with her mother's longer and thicker one. Then, remembering herself, she pulled away and swallowed hard as she met the hot-water witch's eyes.

"I apologise on behalf of my shoal, Re Guiga, for endangering your familiar."

"You hardly called up a vortex storm, girl, unless you've a great deal more power than even this mischief-maker seems to think you do." The witch's eyes were black and shrewd. She stroked a hand over Makini, who was making slow circuits of her neck.

"She's very strong, Guiga," Makini said. "And she worked two original spells, quick and sure in danger conditions."

"Only one of them was original," Tulla muttered. The warning-spell that she'd amplified with the shells had been basic. She had no idea what to make of this. The Re Guiga she'd met had been dismissive, demanding, and not at all prone to these measured silences.

"Hmm," said Re Guiga. Her eyes bore into Tulla for a while longer. Tulla thought, for no particular reason, of that splintering basalt. "You can spare her, Wallarine?"

Tulla's mother squeezed her shoulder. "If she wants to go."

"Go? Where?"

"To the Underwash!" Makini shot forth and nudged himself up against Tulla's chest. "You'll love it there, I've been trying to tell you, it's *so* much better than this lukewarm—"

"That's enough," said Re Guiga. "Let the girl think."

Tulla opened her mouth. Closed it. Opened it. Disbelief bubbled through her fatigue. "Have the last few days been a— a *job interview*?"

"An aptitude test," said Re Guiga. "Though one I never intended to take such a dramatic turn." She took hold of Makini again and gave him a quick, stern shake. "I apologise for endangering *you*, Tullarae, on behalf of my familiar. And I offer you an apprenticeship, if you'll—"

"Yes," blurted Tulla. "Rotting lights, are you serious? Mum, is she—*yes*." To travel north and see new things, to play the tourist herself for once. And to study under this woman who could stop a stormbeast in its tracks!

Re Guiga reached formally for Tulla's hand. She paused, when she had hold of it, and lifted it to sniff. Then she turned her head to Makini, eyebrows raised.

"Why does this girl smell of my own magic?"

"Er," said Makini, ribboning appealingly at Tulla.

"Oh, no," Tulla said firmly. She felt herself grinning, joy a hot current inside her. "*You* get to tell her."

Crash Baby

Donna Maree Hanson

```
TV2 idle mode.
```

Sensors detect ship-wide concussion. Emergency clamps engage. Emergency system shut down . . .

. . .

System start up . . .

System check. Extractor claw arm test. Grip arm test. Secondary multi-function arm test. Auxiliary multifunction arm test. Roller treads test. Normal dexterity confirmed. Audio sensor test.

Whoooop! Whuup! Whoooop! Whuup!

Immediate shut down audio sensors. Auditory overload. Set auto repair. Engage visual and chemical sensors.

Visual sensors confirm hull breach. Chemical sensors detect smoke, ozone, carbon particulates. Zero oxygen.

```
    TV2 attempts to mesh with ship
        command AI . . .

    Attempting to contact ship
        command AI . . .
```

> Attempting to contact ship command
> AI . . . Nil response
>
> Reset . . .
>
> Attempting to contact ship
> command AI . . .
>
> Return message. Ship command
> AI in safe mode.
>
> TV2 to AI. Status update requested.
>
> Ship command AI . . . Nil response.

Commencing visual scan of section 25. Escape pods rows 10 through 15 warning lights flashing. TV2 rolls forward for visual inspection. Escape pods 10 through 13 successfully ejected. Escape pod 14 in situ. Escape pod 15 intact. Access blocked by subflooring from level 24 and higher.

Scan for life signs in escape pod 14. Nil life signs detected. Linking to visual feed. Confirm three deceased humans within.

> TV2 to AI: Three deceased humans in
> pod 14. Status update requested.
>
> Ship command AI . . .

Scanning for life signs in escape pod 15. Inconclusive. Engage visual feed. Inconclusive. Engage audio feed. Sound detected. Unable to identify source. Unable to confirm lifesigns.

> Attempting to contact ship command
> AI . . . Nil response.
>
> Initiate emergency response
> coded commands.

> Auto mode engaged: Command override:
> Protect human life priority one.

TV2 determines sound to be human in origin. TV2 rolls over to escape pod 15. Extends extractor claw to shift debris. Nil achieved. Debris is too heavy for TV2 extractor claw.

> Message to ship command AI. Alert.
> Alert. Assistance required.
>
> Ship command AI . . .

Tries alternate. Searching. Identify Junction 20.

> TV2 to JS20: Assistance required to
> move debris obstructing escape pod
> 15. Human life sign priority.
>
> JS20 to TV2: Command submitted. S20 heavy
> lifter dispatched. Status update?
>
> TV2 to JS20: Hull breach. Zero
> atmosphere in S25. Assume maximum
> casualties. Update from JS20?
>
> JS20 to TV2: Sensors indicate zero
> atmosphere in section 20. Nil
> life signs. Human crew terminated
> or departed via escape pod.
>
> TV2 to JS20: Concur.
> Communication from AI?
>
> JS20 to TV2: No response. Damaged?
>
> TV2 to JS20: Not enough
> information to determine.

Audio detects sound within escape pod 15. Nothing on visual feed. Evidence of human viability. Status unknown.

> TV2 to AI: Detected human life signs
>   in pod 15. Request instructions.
>
> AI to TV2: Segmentation of AI in
>   progress. Dispatching to TV2 unit.

Ship command AI diverting to subsystem TV2. Purging memory to accommodate AI.

> TV2 to AI: Query memory deletion. Routine
>   maintenance is TV2 main function.
>
> AI to TV2: Segmented database
>   requires memory. Memory filled.
>   Engaging expanded memory.

S20 heavy maintenance arrives.

> S20 to TV2: Instructions?
>
> TV2 to S20: Initiate hull seal.
>   Remove debris blocking access
>   to escape pod 15. Advise when
>   atmosphere is replenished.

S20 commences hull repair.

> TV2 to AI: Why did ship command
>   AI relocate to TV2?
>
> AI to TV2: Major damage to ship command
>   station. Memory sections stored
>   remotely in key locations. Human
>   survivor requires detailed database

> to support life functions. TV2
> is responsible for survivor.

TV2 pauses. TV2 digests new information. TV2 has already engaged Protect Human Life protocol.

> AI to TV2: Hull is sealed. Atmosphere
> restored. Ship spin is reengaged
> gravity at .5. Unlock pod
> 15. S20 heavy maintenance
> unit returning to base.

TV2 rolls over to the escape pod door and engages unlock. Sensors locate small human inside.

> AI to TV2: Engage all sensors,
> include olfactory update.

> TV2 to AI: Query olfactory?

> AI to TV2: Necessary when
> dealing with humans.

TV2 reaches into pod with extractor claw arm and grip arm. Small human moves erratically and cries. Olfactory sensors detect strong odour.

> TV2 to AI: What is the odour?
> Does it require action?

> AI to TV2: Searching database. Yes.
> Human is an infant. Requires diaper
> change. Diapers are in emergency
> storage unit 15-1. Unit 15.2 has
> necessary formula for feeding.

TV2 lifts soft, fleshy child that moves continuously. TV2 studies infant with main visual sensor.

```
TV2 to AI: More information
    requested. What is the infant's
    designation? What model is it?

AI to TV2: Searching database. Ship's
    complement contained three children
    under the age of three years. One
    child was six months old. Name
    of child is irretrievable.

TV2 to AI: Irretrievable?

AI to TV2: Data no longer exists.
    Suggest TV2 give name.

TV2 to AI: Did we crash?

AI to TV2: #@$! Insufficient data
    to determine cause of hull
    breach. Crash has same result.

TV2 to AI: Child's designation
    is Crash Baby.

AI to TV2: Good designation. Here
    is data for maintenance of six-
    month-old human child.
```

TV2 receives information. TV2 places Crash Baby on floor and rolls to emergency unit to extract diaper. TV2 returns to infant. Crash Baby cries and thrashes arms and legs. TV2 examines diaper with extractor arm and queries database. Diagram displays method of application. TV2 holds Crash Baby in grip arm and uses extractor claw to undo ties on diaper. Olfactory senses override as TV2 freezes and sensors attempt to analyse.

> AI to TV2: Belay that analysis.
> Crash Baby is moving.

TV2 holds soiled diaper in extractor claw and reclasps Crash Baby in grip arm, using secondary multifunction arm to secure grip. Auxiliary multifunction arm opens diaper beneath crash baby.

> AI to TV2: Soiling exists on Crash
> Baby skin. Employ cleansing arm.

> TV2 to AI: Cleansing arm? All arms
> are currently employed.

> AI to TV2: Try this approach.

AI sends new instructions. TV2 assesses instruction and then holds Crash Baby with grip arm. Dumps soiled diaper on the floor and extends extractor claw arm to maximum length to storage unit to retrieve cleansing wipes. Crash Baby screams. TV 2 retracts extractor claw, employs both secondary multifunction arms while extractor claw deploys cleansing wipes to soiled surface of skin. TV2 flicks soiled wipes on top of soiled diaper. Crash Baby waves arms and legs. TV2 picks up clean diaper and Crash Baby rolls away.

> AI to TV2: Human baby is fragile.

> TV2 to AI: Thank you for
> that observation.

TV2 studies Crash Baby and meshes diagram with image of constantly moving child. Diagram does not show baby in motion. TV2 attempts to compensate. TV2 lifts baby with grip arm and deploys multifunction arms to place diaper over rear end of Crash Baby. Extractor arms engage adhesive tapes.

TV2 lifts baby. Baby squeals.

> TV2 to AI: Did I hurt it?
>
> AI to TV2: Searching database.
> Squeal suggests joy.
>
> TV2 to AI: What is joy?
>
> AI to TV2: When all systems
> are fully functional.

Crash Baby begins to cry and thrash arms and legs. Liquid leaks from its eyeballs. Infant human has soft fuzz on top of head, small fleshy ears and brown eyes and a small pink mouth. However, mouth enlarges when Crash Baby cries.

> TV2 to AI: ?
>
> AI to TV2: Searching database. Noise
> and actions suggest hunger. Child
> formula is in storage unit.

TV2 leaves Crash Baby on the floor. Minor Maintenance Unit 1 glides across floor to scoop up soiled diaper and wipes. Returns to garbage chute.

TV2 extracts premade formula feed tube and engages inbuilt warmer. Returning to Crash Baby, TV2 passes milk to Crash Baby in the grip claw. Crash Baby looks at feeding tube, cries and thrashes arms and legs.

> TV2 to AI: Crash Baby has
> not taken formula.
>
> AI to TV2: Searching database.
> Sending diagram to TV2.

TV2 examines diagram and circles Crash Baby on the floor. If the diaper goes this end then the milk goes in the other. TV2 switches feeding tube to multifunction arm and extends grip and extractor claws to hold Crash Baby at 45 degree angle. Secondary multifunction claw extends feeding tube to Crash Baby's lips. Crash Baby opens mouth and seizes soft end and sucks.

TV2 whirls around and maintains feeding angle. Task successfully completed. Crash Baby keeps drinking. Feeding tube empties and TV2 discards empty tube. Crash Baby cries. TV2 raises Crash Baby so head is level to TV2's main visual sensor. Crash Baby ejects previously ingested milk onto main visual sensor. TV2 shudders and spins.

>   TV2 to AI: Malfunction?
>
>   AI to TV2: Searching database.
>   Regurgitation of feed is
>   within normal parameters.

TV2 deploys secondary multifunction arm to retrieve cleansing wipes to clean main visual sensor.

>   TV2 to AI: What is the next part of
>   the maintenance sequence?
>
>   AI to TV2: Searching database. Child
>   should play and then sleep.
>
>   TV2: Define play.
>
>   AI to TV2: Searching database.
>   Sending diagrams.

TV2 studies diagrams and places Crash Baby on the floor. TV2 retrieves a selection of spare parts from maintenance hold. TV2 rolls cut sections of piping along the floor to Crash Baby. Crash Baby flips from back to front and grabs piping and bangs it on the floor. Crash Baby does not cry while at play.

TV2 studies the next item in the sequence. Sleeping arrangements for Crash Baby. TV2 surveys pile of debris from crash which heavy maintenance has yet to rehouse in the recycling section of Bottom Deck 50. TV2 selects malleable sheeting and bends and twists and deploys secondary multifunction arm to weld joins. Then TV2 rolls over to the storage unit and extracts soft bedding. AI assesses storage unit supplies and advises there is sufficient to keep Crash Baby alive for one earth year. TV2 pauses. A year? TV2 makes up small bed and returns to where Crash Baby is playing. Crash Baby is not there. Sections of piping are there but Crash Baby is not. TV2 starts scanning deck area and detects Crash Baby heading for hole in deck plating near pod 15. Crash Baby slides on stomach and pushes with feet. TV2 rolls over to Crash Baby at maximum speed and deploys grip arm, snatching Crash Baby by the foot and lifts.

```
TV2 to AI: What do I do with
    Crash Baby now?
```

Crash baby emits a squeal as it dangles with head down.

```
AI to TV2: Searching database. Rock
    Crash Baby to sleep mode.

TV2 to AI: !!! Sleep mode?

AI to TV2: Return Crash Baby to
    feed position and rotate your
    torso to create movement.
```

TV2 deploys extractor arm and multifunction arm to support Crash Baby's head while transferring hold from feet. Crash Baby is horizontal. TV2 rotates main body 30 degrees to the right and then 30 degrees to the left. Repeats.

```
AI to TV2: Slow to half speed.
```

TV2 looks down to Crash Baby's face. Dark brown eyes stare up at

TV2. When TV2 slows the rate of rotation, Crash Baby's lips curl into a smile and the skin around the dark brown eyes crinkles. A squeal leaps out of Crash Baby's lips. TV2 assesses that Crash Baby likes being rocked. 1:35:22 later and Crash Baby is still awake.

```
TV2 to AI: This method has not induced
    sleep. Self diagnostic indicates
    systems maintenance is required.

AI to TV2: Yes. Searching for
    alternative methods of sleep
    induction. Sending TV2 a diagram.
```

TV2 examines the diagram. TV2 rolls over to the bed and places Crash Baby on the bedding. Crash Baby grabs bottom claw of extractor arm and speaks.

TV2 listens but cannot understand. Crash Baby pulls on bottom extractor claw and puts in mouth. TV2 decides not to ask AI for instruction. Instead, TV2 uses tip of grip arm to sooth Crash Baby's fuzzy head. Crash Baby's eyes close. TV2 draws extractor claw out of reach. TV2 rolls backwards and then turns torso to face recharge niche. Crash Baby cries out. TV2 stops, rotates top level with visual sensor. Crash Baby is sleeping. TV2 slips into recharge niche and commences routine system maintenance and recharge of main battery

This cycle repeats. Crash Baby continues to grow. TV2 spends all day maintaining Crash Baby, until TV2's own systems begin to fail. Many times TV2 is pulled from recharging and routine maintenance to attend Crash Baby's bodily functions. TV2 is adept at holding Crash Baby in many positions and knows which positions make Crash Baby squeal with joy. However, over time these tactics are insufficient to distract Crash Baby.

```
TV2 to AI: Crash Baby maintenance
```

> schedule is insufficient.
> Request new parameters.
>
> AI to TV2: Searching database.

Sends stream of text to TV2. TV2 reads texts and responds.

> TV2 to AI: Crash Baby requires
> weaning to solid food. This takes
> many cycles to accomplish.
>
> AI to TV2: Food sachets are
> in the supply unit.

TV2 extracts a food sachet, a small pocket filled with a soft substance. TV2 compares it to the list of first foods on list supplied by AI and exchanges it for another, then another until rice porridge is found. TV2 heads to where Crash Baby is playing with pipe sections in bed. TV2 examines Crash Baby and evaluates how to best insert food sachet into Crash Baby. TV2 takes off lid to the small spout and extends extractor claw with spout facing out. Crash Baby smiles and squeals and swats at food sachet. From the impact, thick white liquid squirts into Crash Baby's face. Crash Baby screams. TV2 rolls backward and grabs cleansing wipes and returns. Crash Baby wriggles and squeals as TV2 tries to remove thick white liquid from eyes and mouth and right ear. Crash Baby stops crying and TV2 tries again. Slowly, slowly, TV2 extends the sachet. Crash Baby watches with big brown eyes. Big brown eyes turn in as sachet approaches mouth.

> AI to TV2: You need to talk
> to Crash Baby.
>
> TV2 to AI: Talk? What talk?
>
> AI to TV2: Human language.
>
> TV2 to AI: Which language?

    AI to TV2: It does not matter.

TV2 has not been programmed to speak any human language but does not supply this information. TV2 says to Crash Baby. Open your mouth. It comes out as a bit of static with a high-pitched whine on the end. That's TV2's language. AI volunteers no further advice. TV2 speaks again and offers the food sachet. Crash Baby sucks on the small tube and swallows the porridge. Crash Baby stops, pushes sachet away and spits up porridge onto bedding and then cries.

    AI to TV2: There is a problem
         with your technique.

    TV2 to AI: Do you wish to take over?

    AI to TV2: I have no body.

    TV2 to AI: That is convenient for you.

TV2 perseveres with the food sachets and milk tubes as instructed by AI. Each rotation Crash Baby takes more food and different types of food.

Eventually, Crash Baby snatches food sachets from TV2's extractor arm and sucks the food out without being encouraged. TV2 assesses this as a good outcome.

Crash Baby increases in size. Crash baby does more frequent soiling of diapers. The next size of diapers is required. TV2 wishes that AI had a body as TV2 is constantly undercharged and lacking basic system maintenance. Every time TV2 enters the recharge niche and commences system maintenance, Crash Baby is either extruding liquid from either end and once both ends at the same time. TV2 recalls a malfunction. TV2 experienced an indecision paradox. It could not decide to deal with the front end extrusion or the back end extrusion and TV2 went round in circles for ten minutes until AI made a decision.

> AI to TV2: Uploading language files. Crash Baby needs to develop language skills. TV2 you need to talk to Crash Baby, explain the world in which it exists and tell it stories.
>
> TV2 to AI: This is something you could do. You could channel your vocal output to the intercom grill that humans used to use.
>
> AI to TV2: It would be much easier for you to do it. Crash Baby has bonded with you.
>
> TV2 to AI: Bonded? What is bonded?
>
> AI to TV2: It is when all parts are in harmony and work well together to achieve optimum performance.

TV2 considers this information but cannot parse it.

> TV2 to AI: Do you mean that if a part is missing from the whole it would notice the missing part and not function optimally?
>
> AI to TV2: You have it!

TV2 rolled over to Crash Baby's bed and accessed the language files. How are you Crash Baby? Static, squeak, high-pitched squeal. Crash Baby laughs and tries to grab onto TV2's extractor claw.

"Are you functioning well?"

More giggles.

TV2 to AI: It is not working. Crash
	Baby is not communicating.

AI to TV2: It takes time. You need
	to talk to Crash Baby for months
	and months before Crash Baby can
	communicate in return. Language
	skills are acquired over time. Small
	words, then sentences. Crash Baby
	needs to hear complete sentences
	in order to speak properly. Crash
	Baby is depending on you.

TV2 to AI: You would be better
	at this than me.

AI to TV2: I am busy. I have
	been repairing the ship's
	database. It takes a lot of
	my processing capacity.

TV2 turns back to Crash Baby and says in ship standard language. "This is the ship *Strident*. We were hulled near Cutty Five. Humans either escaped or were killed. You are the only survivor on board. This is section 25 and you were found in escape pod 15. We do not know your name so we call you Crash Baby."

Crash Baby throws out the pipe segments and they crash to the floor. TV2 notes this and picks them up. "It is wrong to throw your toys, Crash. Are you sleepy yet?"

TV2's battery charge is at 35 percent, which is not an optimal capacity. If only Crash would sleep, TV2 could go for a recharge. Crash Baby crawls out of the bed and swims across the floor. TV2 engages language files again." Crash come back here. Crash you need to sleep now. Crash do not go near that hole in the deck." TV2 sends request to heavy maintenance unit to seal up hole. Now that Crash Baby is mobile, TV2 assesses that hole in decking represents danger to human life and must take priority.

TV2 rolls over to pick up Crash Baby by body suit. TV2 assess that body suit would be better designed with handle to make grabbing Crash Baby easier. TV2 turns Crash Baby around. "Come this way."

TV2 backs up and hopes that Crash will follow. Crash turns back to hole in decking. TV2 tries another tactic. Accessing story file: *Jack and the Beanstalk*. TV2 picks up Crash and takes the baby to bed. TV2 recounts the tale of *Jack and the Beanstalk*. Crash Baby listens with wide brown eyes and mouth pursed, fingers clasping and unclasping TV2's extractor claw. Crash pushes against the restraining arm and starts to grunt and yell. TV2 releases hold on Crash. Crash crawls out of bed and heads back to the hole in the deck. TV2 has resentful thoughts about AI as TV2 rolls back over to prevent Crash from falling through the hole.

```
JS20 to TV2: S25 floor repair is
    not a system priority. Seek
    priority rating from AI.
```

A noise alerts TV2 while in the recharge niche. With regret, TV2 notes battery is only at 73 percent charge. Sensor sweep reveals that Crash Baby is not in bed. TV2 launches from the recharge niche. "Crash! Crash!" TV2 calls while sweeping into the centre of the room. A sense of foreboding builds in TV2. The hole is still there in the floor. TV2 glides over and there dangling from a sharp piece of metal plating is Crash Baby, a piece of body suit snagged on the metal. TV2 refrains from expressing dismay in language and extends the grip arm to secure the child.

```
TV2 to AI: Crash Baby in danger
```

> of death. Request repairs to
> decking immediately. TV2 sending
> image of Crash dangling from
> the destroyed decking.
>
> AI to TV2: Acknowledged. Heavy
> maintenance unit dispatched.

TV2 places Crash Baby on the floor. Crash Baby grabs onto TV2's grip and extractor arms and bounces on two feet. This is a new action from Crash Baby, but TV2 is not sure if AI should be informed. TV2 should request direct access to database. TV2 does all the work in maintaining Crash Baby.

More time passes and Crash Baby does new things each rotation. Crash Baby can clap hands. TV2 sings songs to Crash Baby and Crash Baby laughs. TV2 finds the sound of Crash Baby's laugh increases internal harmonics.

This cycle TV2 starts the rotation with a full charge. TV2 cannot remember the last time with a full charge. TV2 is still contemplating full charge then notices Crash Baby is not in bed. TV2 engages visual senses and finds Crash Baby on feet and holding onto wall for support.

> TV2 to AI: Sending image. Request update
> to Crash Baby maintenance routine.
>
> AI to TV2: Crash Baby is
> starting to walk.
>
> TV2 to AI: Walk? Crash Baby has not
> made talking a priority.
>
> AI to TV2: You need to talk
> to Crash Baby more.

TV2 rolls close to Crash Baby. Crash Baby transfers hands to TV2's main carapace. "Crash Baby walk to TV2?"

"Eee," Crash Baby says.

> TV2 to AI: Crash Baby said
> "eee". Is this a word?
>
> AI to TV2: It is a pre-word.

TV2 tries to get Crash Baby to walk and ponders what "eee" means. It could be that Crash Baby is trying to say TV2. TV2 purges that thought as being illogical.

Every rotation Crash Baby gets better at standing and trying to walk. TV2 watches as Crash Baby stands, slowing unbending knees. Then Crash Baby lifts a foot and falls down onto rear. Crash Baby eyebrows move up and down. TV2 thinks this is language too. TV2 likes Crash Baby's eyebrows.

Then Crash Baby tries again. "TV2 help Crash Baby?"

Crash Baby looks up to TV2. "Eeee" and then falls down.

TV2's battery needs recharging, but Crash Baby does not sleep as much as previously. TV2 has to snatch periods of recharge and system maintenance when Crash Baby sleeps.

> AI to TV2: Alert! Alert!

TV2 surges from recharge niche.

> TV2 to AI: What is wrong with Crash Baby?

Immediately, TV2 sees that Crash Baby is asleep in bed and halts forward movement.

> AI to TV2: Rescue ship is on course
> and decelerating. Expected arrival
> in thirty-one rotations.
>
> TV2 to AI: Rescue ship coming
> for Crash Baby?

> AI to TV2: Confirmed. Then, rescue
> ship will recover other survivors
> who made it to planet Cutty
> Five in the escape pods.

TV2 rolls forward to look at Crash Baby while sleeping. The fuzz on Crash Baby's head has turned into dark hair. Crash Baby's little pink mouth smiles while sleeping. TV2 experiences intrasystem harmonic. All TV2's systems are functioning well together. TV2 ponders if this is "joy".

Crash Baby wakes and climbs out of the bed. Crash Baby tries to stand. Crash Baby is upright and stepping forward. Crash Baby puts out arms to TV2 and walks a few wobbly steps. TV2 assesses danger of falling at 99 percent certain. Crash Baby keeps coming and clasps TV2. "Eeee."

TV2 experiences strange sensation in central processing unit. More than an intrasystem harmonic. TV2 cannot categorise this occurrence.

> TV2 to AI: Reporting malfunction.

> AI to TV2: Send systems diagnostic.

TV2 sends diagnostic.

> AI to TV2: Give me visual feed.

TV2 connects AI to visual feed. Crash Baby pushes away from TV2 and wobbles toward the bed. Crash Baby falls down with a splat. AI makes strange noises. "Her, her, her."

> TV2 to AI: What is that sound?

> AI to TV2: That is laughter. Crash Baby's
> attempts at walking are funny.

TV2 does not understand funny. TV2 experiences strange sensation in central processing unit.

Crash Baby's walking improves and fat little legs carry it all around Section 20. The recharge niche becomes Crash Baby's favourite hiding place. "Eeee!"

```
AI to TV2: Rescue ship docking. Prepare
          Crash Baby for departure.
```

TV2 follows orders and prepares emergency food stores and clothing for Crash Baby's journey. Humans enter through airlock. "It's a baby!" one calls out and bounds over to pick up Crash Baby. Crash Baby wiggles and tries to get down. The human puts Crash Baby on the ground. Crash Baby walks over to TV2. "Eee Bee."

TV2 swivels 45 degrees to the right and then to the left.

```
AI to TV2: What are you doing?

TV2 to AI: I am not sure.

AI to TV2: How can you not be
          sure? What happened?
```

Crash Baby reaches TV2 and squashes face against TV2's metal plating. "Eee bee."

The human comes forward. "Thank you for looking after the baby. You've done a great job. We'll take good care of the baby now."

TV2 rolls backwards. Crash Baby holds out arms and cries. "Eee bee. EEE! BEE!"

Another human strokes Crash Baby's back. "It's okay. We will look after you."

Crash Baby turns to TV2 and lifts arms up. "Eee Bee."

TV2 uses extractor claw to stroke Crash Baby's head. Then TV2 swivels and enters the recharge niche. Internal system maintenance commences. TV2 can hear Crash Baby calling "Eee Bee Two."

TV2 experiences strange sensation in central processing unit. This TV2 names a glitch.

        AI to TV2: Status report.

        TV2 . . .

        AI to TV2: Status report!

        TV2 to AI: Crash Baby gone.

        AI to TV2: Did you hear Crash
            Baby say your name?

        TV2 to AI: Eee bee two.

Seriously strange and unidentifiable sensation in the central processing unit.

The Lovers

Matthew Farrer

NOBODY COMES NEAR the house. Something about him stops them. He lives with the cicadas and the flies. He can hear the soft scuffle of spiders in the corners and the busy scratch of the centipedes and beetles beneath the floor. He perceives the way the heat desiccates the eucalyptus leaves to a hot crackle and shimmers off the galvanised-iron corrugations of the roof. The birdsong is always distant. They won't come in view of the house, won't even fly overhead. He can't ever remember seeing a real bird, only pictures.

He doesn't remember how he got the house, or if anyone owned it before him. It looks old; older than most of the people in the little town, but he doesn't know how old he is himself.

He keeps the place respectable, as far as he can understand the term. It's important to him to think that if anyone from the town might stumble on the place some day they will find it neat and normal and with nothing awry. He owns clothes he tries hard to keep neat and clean, although it can be hard to remember which ones are for what, and holding the right shape to wear them takes concentration.

He has food. He can simply stand outside the house and dig his toes deeper and deeper into the soil. Sometimes, as a treat, he will flit along the town's streets and find a well-composted garden bed to crouch in, or wander through the landfill to the west, or the graveyard to the north, stopping every so often to grip the ground and draw up its beautiful nutrients.

He only rarely needs to catch things to eat, these days. Sometimes when he is in desperate need of strength, he will send his attention toward where he can feel some animal rustling in the woods: lizards, sometimes snakes, once or twice a young kangaroo. He snags them with that attention and drags them in. Underneath the house is a layer of entangled white bones. He sometimes frets about whether to get rid of them, but never really does anything. He is fairly sure none of the bones are human, but every so often he can't remember how sure he is and has to rummage through them to see, to stop himself from fretting.

He can read. He pieced the skills together by hiding in the scrub at the edge of the schoolyard year after year, and carefully directing his senses into the rooms where the teachers were talking. He could not keep it up for long; after a few minutes of his attention the children's noses would bleed and the teacher would stammer and he would slink away, ashamed.

He has read every book in the library, holding his shape by sheer will — no matter how it hurts. He watches television through windows and steals newspapers. But no answer, never even a clue to what he wants:

"What am I?"

———

A football team from some district a half-day's drive away has come to town for a match play, and that night there is a fight at the pub. He is crouched against the wall of the garage one street over, where he can stay out of sight in the shadow and smell of the rubbish skips. He rocks back and forward and memorises the sounds. Shouting. Boots on gravel. Boots on concrete. Flesh hitting flesh, flesh hitting wood. Something breaks, sharp and shrill, shattering glass. A bottle? He has sniffed and licked broken bottles in the landfill, but whatever it is that is interesting about them remains beyond him.

He is repeating each word he hears under his breath, feeling the sounds, when she sneaks up on him. He only registers the sound of her footsteps when she is far closer than she should have gotten. He flattens and snakes under a skip, watching her. She should have seen him, but she has not.

She is walking a little unsteadily, and her eyes are just a little unfocused. She is breathing just a little harshly. These are cold nights, this time of year, and he can see her breath in the orange backlight of the street lamp she is walking past. Her heels click and clack on the concrete.

He pulls back into himself, like a timid human yanking a hand back from a spider. Brushing too close to him hurts people. He hates himself for that, the shame is hot and acrid every time his carelessness leaves someone marred by his presence. He must have hurt this one. He is sure he can see the aftershock of him in her blankness. Her . . . strangeness.

Once she is well past, he ghosts across the street to be directly behind her, then turns his back on her and goes in the direction from which she came, pouring himself through the empty intersections and shadowy vacant lots. He doesn't know what he is looking for until he sees it.

Swaying at the edge of the storm-drain culvert is an ungainly stack of town-fringe debris. Two mismatched truck tyres are piled on one another. An empty oil drum teeters on top. Its top has been stuffed with broken plastic in what would be gaudy colours in any light but the sodium orange of the streetlamps. A shabby plastic Christmas tree has been jammed into the bin as a top-piece.

He has made similar things—stacks, patterns, grooves—when he has been occupied or nervous. If he knew of people's habits of unconsciously scrawling doodles or unbending and re-bending paper clips as a nervous tic, he would understand instantly.

He doesn't remember making this. He has not been this way in days. But she . . .

He doesn't know what to think except that he feels afraid. He arrows straight for home, booming through the town so that the men still throwing tired, token punches outside the pub all flinch and look at the sky. They decide it must have been a jet flying low, although none of them can quite believe it, and they make an uneven, slouching pack back inside to drop against the bar and reach for another glass.

—

He has no experience to guide him, and not even any instinct. This is when he feels the spaces most keenly. The gaps in his knowledge filled with strange things he can't name; the roaring emptiness that makes a moat between him and anything he might try to use for help. He has nothing to do but think. But all there is to think about is how helpless he is to handle what he just saw.

He sits in the largest room of the little house in the clearing, motionless, his agitation sloughing off and deforming the floor and walls around him. Outside, in the dark, the trees creak and sob in the still night air.

A night and a day and a night and a day and a night and finally he feels brave enough to leave the house and creep slowly toward the town once more. He doesn't use the road (or it was once a road, now two stony wheel-tracks almost invisible beneath wiry, green-yellow weeds), but seeps slowly through the woodland like a chemical spill through the earth.

He weaves as best he can between the houses on the two-acre blocks at the town fringes, and he is not seen, although once he ventures too close to a hen-house and two of the birds go spinning across their yard, screaming and caroming off the sagging wire fences, until after he has passed they fall dead with blood-filled eyes. At another house he hears the loud chuff of static interference and angry words, an adult's and a teenager's, as his passage drowns out a television transmission and scrambles hard drives and phones. He cringes away from the anger he feels in the house, wraps himself into a ball and drops away into the thickest greenery he can find until he feels himself covered.

No excuses, he tells himself. No carelessness just because . . . just because.

Activity in the town's broad main thoroughfare, and in the machine shops by the highway turnoff and in the loading yards where the wheat silos rear up over the railway. He avoids it all, bellying along drainage ditches, stopping in empty lots to listen, forcing his shape so he can walk the quietest streets and scent the air.

Before he finds anything, he is found.

He is lying on his back in the exact centre of the cricket oval at the town's northwest edge, looking straight up into the sky, almost calm enough to start relaxing his shape, when something brushes his senses, as soft but as definite as a breeze, as leaves trailing along his skin. His body wrenches as he catches and stops the urge to leap up, and he makes himself lie flat. Cautiously, cautiously . . .

And then all his senses seem to curdle. Every perception crimps as though in the grip of pliers, distorts into pain that lances back into him so even his own sense of himself, of the body he controls so utterly, becomes a violation. He screams, once, briefly, before he bites down and swallows his voice, but that split-second is still enough to kill and desiccate the grass in a three-metre circle around him and send cracks running along the drying earth, from where he sits almost to the boundary line. He rolls on the crisp dead stuff, panicked and angry. He has never wanted to lash out before, but that impulse is in his brain as perfectly-formed as though he had trained it there.

After a moment, it passes.

After another moment, the thought arrives.

I didn't mean it. I'm sorry.

It is faster and more fluidly integrated than a strung-together sequence of words, but not quite a pure thought. He does not . . . know . . .

Before he has consciously formed the intent he has flung his thoughts outward, the direction half-random, groping out among the echoes and the life-smells for what just touched him. His awareness splinters the wooden fence around the ground, passes through the pavilion where the windows craze with cracks and the water instantly boils in the tank that feeds the change-room showers.

There's a trace of something, a gauzy half-seen thing, a lacy shawl whipped back in slipstream, gone as he closes his grip about it. He shouts after it, and the two trucks parked outside the haulage depot rock on their tyres as their windows blow out and their fuel tanks go in ripe orange bursts of fire.

—

He stays to watch as the people run out, and watches some more as the fire trucks arrive, the police cars, the curious spectators. He makes his shape and walks by the fringes of the crowd, holding himself in tightly so he won't hurt the people clustering up and down the street. He wonders if any will turn around and look at him; will point, tell each other look, look at that, there's a stranger here. A few days ago, the fear of it would have sent him away. Now, he finds he has other things on his mind.

He waits long enough to make sure there is nobody hurt, although he cannot imagine what he would do if there were. Then he walks to the edges of the town, beyond them, lets his shape go with a small sigh of relief and moves back along the way he came.

I don't want you to be afraid of me.

The thought comes the way the earlier one did, and before he can really register its arrival he has replied, *I know you didn't mean it. I don't want to hurt you either.*

He stands among the trees for some time, waiting for more, but all he can feel is a faint taste of gratitude, and that could just be his imagination.

—

The thought that comes to him while he sits in the central corridor of his house in the blowy late evening is that they do not want to hurt each other, and they do not have to. He knows how not to hurt the people in the town. Keep his shape tight so nobody properly sees him. Keep all but the crudest of his senses folded inward so that their touch doesn't cause pain. Never do more than whisper so that, so that . . .

But he doesn't have to do this with . . .

He didn't hold himself in. He didn't control his words and take care to make them in only the lowest, quietest way that didn't hurt. He hadn't been careful.

He had still heard, and spoken.

It had hurt at first because he hadn't known. But not later.

There was a way to do this. There was a way. A different way he could be.

He wonders what they will talk about next.

—

Have you always been here? he asks. He wonders what it will feel like to know there has been someone else in the town along with him, a life laid out side-by-side to his own, beyond his vision until now.

No, she says. *I . . . moved. Travelled.* He sees, tastes, remembers fragments as she breathes them out to him. Running across bare red earth beneath the sun. Walking along train tracks, watching them tarnish beneath her. The landscape changes. Scrub. Grass. Trees. A town.

He senses curiosity.

I have always been here. I think. I don't know where I came from.

Nor do I, she says, *but I think that's how we are. We don't need that the way they do.* He feels the shift in her attention, as though he had his arms around her and she had shifted about in his grip. She is looking out from the hilltop where she is standing, out over the town. He shifts uncomfortably in among the granite boulders (he is on a different hilltop, eight kilometres away, west-south-west of the town to her south-south-east), but her gaze is light and distracted, not intense enough to hurt anyone.

I have never needed to know, she goes on. *Even when I wanted to, I realised I didn't need to. They need to care. I don't think we do. I don't. The other one didn't.*

It takes him a moment, but when it properly takes hold the thought lights him up. The day is overcast and blustering but the rocks around him grow as warm as a lazy spring afternoon.

The other one? Another one? Like us?

There is no leak of senses and memories this time. She is guarded.

He wasn't like us.

But if he looked, moved . . . I mean, if he had our nature! How many of us are there? I have spent years not knowing, I can't count them. You can't not tell me, please, not now.

He wasn't like us, she says again. *He didn't have our nature.* His frustration rolls off the hilltop like a wave, freezing the little grass-living animals with fear and sending insects into a frenzy. *Oh, he was made like us,* she goes on. *But he wasn't like us. And it doesn't matter. I shouldn't have told you. It doesn't matter.*

I don't understand, he says, because it doesn't occur to him not to admit it.

He's dead, she says, and as the linked thought comes tumbling through their connection he knows she wanted to stop herself saying it, and he knows she is quietly, treacherously glad that it is out.

I killed him.

—

An afternoon and a day and a night and he is shivering in the dark although the night is warm. There is a wound in the tree line where he came home through the woodland, crying in panic, shoving the trees aside, needing to be inside his walls. It took him hours to think that she could easily follow him, and that then not only he himself would be in danger but this home he had made. Somehow the idea of endangering the house he has taken such care of is just as frightening as . . .

She had killed him. The other one, before she came here. Killed him.

He didn't give her a chance to say why. He had been gone as soon as he understood the words. She had killed him. There had been two others like him, now there was one. What if there were no more of them? What if she wanted them all dead? What if she came here and found him?

He should never have gone looking for her. That first terrifying brush of their senses on the grass of the cricket ground should have warned him.

He strokes the linoleum floor for comfort, and tries to count and calm the pulses and slams of his body, so different to what the people in the town have, so familiar to him even so.

He thinks it's starting to work, finally, that he's starting to calm and can think about what to do next. He can't imagine fleeing the town, can't conceive of fighting her.

All imagining is driven out of his mind when he hears her in the trail he left through the trees, coming toward him, calling softly.

—

He bursts out of the far side of the house, and that is precisely what happens: the side of the building that held the two small bedrooms and the closets explodes outward as though a truck had barrelled out of some secret door and then through the walls. At the far side of the clearing he stops and turns, backing slowly toward the overgrown track, watching for her.

You don't understand, she tells him. He can make her out beyond the house. *You don't understand. I want you to understand.*

You killed him, he answers, *and when you've killed me who will you go on to kill? I thought I was the only one of us. How can you want that for yourself? To be the only one?*

She doesn't answer straight away. She moves into the clearing. He shifts a little to keep the ruins of the house between them. She lets him.

When I said he didn't have our nature, I didn't mean his form wasn't ours. *In that way, he could have been your twin.* He waits, trembling, for her to go on. *He didn't have your nature, or mine.*

I don't understand.

Think of the first things we told each other. That we didn't mean to hurt each other. That we were sorry we had. That we wanted to trust each other. That wasn't his nature.

He grapples hard with this.

Think of what we do to them, she says, coming closer. *Think of what we did to each other at first. What we can do to each other if we're not careful.*

He remembers all too well. The ghost of the pain from when their senses first touched ripples along the edge of his perceptions again. There is a shimmer-flash of heat around him as the feedback from the sense-memory briefly boils the air. He backs away from her a little more.

Here, she says. *Come and walk with me.*

It takes him time, but the moon goes behind a cloud and the gloom gives him the courage to follow her away.

—

Not a word passes between them while they move through the trees, their paths neatly parallel but separated by stands of forest and folds of land. The moonlight comes, goes. Eventually orange and yellow-white lights start to sprinkle the night ahead of them. They slip into the town together, each moving down a different street. The effort of forming words to her while holding in his shape is cruel.

We can hurt each other, he said. *Was that what you did? How you did it?*

She doesn't answer him but he can feel the churn in her thoughts as she keeps pace. Dogs start to howl nearby and blue light spills out of windows as televisions switch themselves on and spill bright blaring static into empty front rooms.

I didn't want it, she says at last. *It was him that wanted that. You hate that you hurt. He liked it.*

I hate that I hurt. The memories unfold out of one another. The smothering summers and brittle winters curled in his empty house. Moving through the town like a balloon in a crosswind, this way and that, tortuously aware, every moment, of the distance between him and the nearest person to him. Keening to the woods in exhaustion and confusion at the end of a day of it, the insects keening back.

Do you trust me? she asks. They are standing less than fifty metres apart, nothing but air between them. The streets they have been walking down end here in a park and a memorial grove. Over the eastern horizon, the darkness has started to fray and dissolve.

He turns his senses back down the street he had walked so carefully this morning, and even with all his effort the pavement is dimpled and house windows clouded as if with cataracts. Then he looks at the path that she has walked to stand beside him.

She has not guarded herself at all. The pavement smokes and bubbles where she has stepped. The misshapen hulk of a car parked in a driveway now lies on its side on the kerb, its whole body distended as if it had been drawn on wet glass and then smeared out. There is a shape behind the crinkled glass of the windshield and blood is pooling underneath it. A power line that hangs over the street is whirling like a jump-rope. It is exhilarating.

He can feel her thoughts thrumming in him, wordless, as he feels his own awareness folding around her.

We are different to him. We are different to them.

He looks at her. She does not hurt his senses now, even with neither of them being careful, and he feels no pain running back along hers.

We are alike, he says. It seems a simple enough thing. It is all he can think to say.

The reaching out is done by millimetres and paused, uncertain breaths, the distance between skin and skin seeming to close in geological time. Air molecules buzz and thrum furiously in the little space where their fingertips will meet.

Finally, they touch.

—

Everything breaks.

—

These days he likes to dart up to the top of the marble-faced war memorial obelisk at the end of the main street, perch there and look out over the town. They like to stroll up and down the main street together, enjoying the moods of the weather and the seasons. Their repeated passage has remade the asphalt and concrete and grassed islands, left their unmistakable mark on it. It is satisfying to look and think about making this place his home.

The trees along the main street are splintered stumps, but the flower planters along its sides have grown feverishly. The flowers riot and shout with colour, bigger than the span of a big man's hand and their petals able to grip just as brutally hard. Sap and syrup drip from the blooms and run down stems thick as a forearm, among quivering, spine-fringed leaves.

Two bodies lie face down in one of the flower beds nearest his vantage point. He doesn't know who they were. They have been there for some time now.

In the middle of the street a farm truck stands on its nose, the back of its chassis peeled apart like fruit, broken glass from the shop windows piled in drifts against its sides. They had played a game, a courting fancy, making gifts for one another, and this had been one of his to her.

Power poles lean askew over the streets. On that first night their conjoined cries earthed themselves in the wires, wrenched cables out of mounts and knocked down pylons. Ever since, the only light to come to the town has been the sun's. Now that the fires have burned themselves out.

She is sitting astride the street halfway down its length, looking back at him, the force of their love thrumming in the air, potent enough to set the corpses in the buildings around them twitching and jittering. Every so often their thoughts will pass through another orbit of wordless devotion, and the bronze statue of the returning soldier that stands in the middle of the town's roundabout vibrates and softens, another rivulet of molten sweat running down the deforming face.

Brick and concrete alike are crumbling. Shoots and weeds are already pushing up through the surface of the side streets. The animals are gone; some of the insects have died; others are thriving. A centipede big as an adult snake moves out of an overturned and burned-out car and makes its claw-clattering way along the eroded gutter.

There are no words this bright afternoon. They are content to let the breeze and the soft noises of animals be their conversation. They are resting, and preparing. There is nothing to say, nothing to do but bask in each other and wait.

What a wonderful place this will become once the children are born.

Meet Me at the Medusa

Tansy Rayner Roberts

W E ALL HAVE snakes for hair. Some conceal them below wigs and hats. Some stay inside, never venturing out to be seen, and judged, in public. Some wear them proudly, spilling over crisp white collars and leather jackets.

Did you see Ann Veronica in Vogue last week? Designer sunglasses blocking out the light, and serpents trailing down her shoulders over the very latest boho silk sheath cape. She looked a million dollars. She looked exactly like she didn't care that her hair was hissing at the camera.

I have never felt so represented.

I have never felt so scared.

—

There was a time, not so long ago, when none of us could be seen in public. We met at the Medusa, a private club for ladies like us (and not like us). There and only there could we be free to let our snakes fall where they might; though we still covered our eyes with sunglasses as a matter of public safety.

I turned the first man I ever loved to stone. At the Medusa, surrounded by my people, I know that every single one of them has a similar story.

We are not alone. We are not monsters.

We all have snakes for hair.

We all have snakes for hair. And yes, that does not only mean upon our heads. Shaving is not an option; waxing can be done with discretion and a delicate touch. But we don't all have the budget for a private beautician, or even to visit a salon that caters to monsters like us.

At the Medusa, in one of the back rooms of the bar, Amelia comes twice a week to service our needs.

Every tiny snake pulled from its roots survives, under her care. I once stood on the balcony at the back of the club, looking over the yard as she released them, one by one, into the wild.

Ada is the concierge at the Medusa. She's not one of my kind — not a gorgon (yes, I whisper the word if I must say it at all, I still remember the centuries when they came after us with swords). Membership of the Medusa is open to a wide variety of monsters, each more gorgeous and dangerous and secretive than the next.

I don't know what Ada is, but I know I want to be her when I grow up.

Ada can get you anything you need. If you're a member, she has your back. Whether it's a tank full of spiders to eat, an inconvenient corpse to disappear, or tickets to *Hamilton*, Ada can make it happen.

I once saw her face down a dragon, eight-foot high, in the Periwinkle Tea Room on the third floor. The dragon went from wanting to burn the whole place to the ground, to sobbing on Ada's shoulder about how her girlfriend dumped her for a harpy.

I ran into Ada once, outside the club. She was standing in a queue for a taxi, looking sad and grim. In the daylight, her complexion is not the flawless china surface that it appears to be inside the walls of the Medusa.

People were staring. As I got closer, my snakes concealed beneath an over-sized beret, I stared too. I couldn't help it. She had shapes writhing beneath the paleness of her skin. Tentacles, I realised, as I looked closer. Dark shadows of the sea. And scales, not dragon scales, but something altogether more… sinister.

I caught her eye as my path crossed hers, brave enough to offer a friendly smile. I'm trying to be better about these things.

Ada smiled back.

Not all snakes are literal.

—

The monthly meeting of the Snakes For Hair Book Club is held in the Peacock Parlour, on the second floor of the Medusa. A closed session, gorgons only, so that we can let our hair down both literally and figuratively as we read Ovid in translation, Christina Rossetti, Theodora Goss.

A naga recently applied for membership, on the grounds that she feels she is snake enough to join us as we discuss the fierce works of our favourite writers: Mary Shelley, Octavia Butler, Jeanette Ng.

It does not feel comfortable to exclude her, and yet, and yet.

(We have not yet made a resolution about her application.)

Membership of the Medusa does not require an annual subscription — and thank goodness for that, or most of us would be priced out of its beautiful, antique rooms. As it is, I barely have the budget to pay for my own drinks, one weekend a month.

You must be sponsored by an existing member to join. And of course, you must disclose your nature to the President, currently a sleek mermaid who holds her meetings in the large subterranean indoor pool, three floors beneath ground level.

On the day I arrived, thirty-four years old and shaking in my boots, I was guided to the pool by my sponsor, Madame Marie, who chose to mentor me when I first arrived at the laboratory with my new by-correspondence biology degree.

"Trust her and tell the truth," Madame M said at the pool's edge, removing my sunglasses from my eyes and putting them on top of her own head, which writhed and hissed.

I removed my clothes, my boots, my layers of disguise. Naked, with snakes that fell from my scalp past my shoulders, I stepped into the pool.

The water writhed, and bubbled. There were creatures in here with us, dark and shadowed. One of them brushed my leg. I did not scream. Who was I to judge?

The mermaid emerged from the water, hair slicked back, breasts bare. Scales covered her from her hairline all the way down. She met my gaze with her own, and she did not turn to stone.

"Why do you want to be a member of the Medusa Club?" she asked.

I could have said many things. Of how much I had heard of the club and its discreet facilities. That I wanted to be a scientist, and so many of my heroes were members here.

Instead, I went with simplicity. "I want to be with my kind. I want to learn how to take pride in being a monster."

The mermaid smiled. "Welcome to the Medusa," she said, and reached out her scaled fingers to stroke my snakes, like a grandmother tidying me before a public appearance. "You will find friends here. And we have an excellent therapist on retainer."

—

Snakes for hair.

Sometimes it's a metaphor.

Sometimes it's not.

Sometimes it's a cocktail: Snakes For Hair is my favourite listing on the drinks menu in the Banshee Bar, all Kahlua and vodka and mint chip ice cream.

Sometimes it's a way of life.

Sometimes it's a secret password.

Sometimes… it's the truest thing anyone has ever said to me.

—

Meet me at the Medusa one day soon. I'll buy you a drink and show you around. I think you will enjoy the visit.

We all have snakes for hair.

About the Authors

Joanne Anderton is an Australian author who, until recently, was living and working in Japan. Her spec-fic includes the novels *Debris*, *Suited* and *Guardian*, and the short story collection *The Bone Chime Song and Other Stories*. She has won multiple awards including the Aurealis, Ditmar and Australian Shadows Award. Her children's picture book *The Flying Optometrist* was a CBCA notable book, and her non-fiction has been published in *Island Magazine* and *Meanjin*. You can find her online at joanneanderton.com.

—

Grace Chan (gracechanwrites.com) is an Aurealis and Norma K Hemming Award-nominated speculative fiction writer and doctor. Her family migrated from Malaysia to Australia before her first birthday. She writes near-future science fiction about medical technology, far-future voyages to strange worlds and psychological horror where the real and the unconscious bleed together.

Her debut novel, *Every Version of You*, will be published by Affirm Press in 2022.

Her short fiction can be found in *Clarkesworld, Going Down Swinging, Aurealis, Andromeda Spaceways Magazine, Verge: Uncanny* and other places.

—

Matthew Farrer lives in Canberra and is a life member of the CSFG. He has published stories with the Black Library, Fantasy Flight and Twelfth Planet Press. This is his second appearance in a CSFG anthology.

—

DL Fleming is a writer based in Canberra, Australia.

Deborah has a BA and MA in professional communications and has worked in education policy and communication roles. In the past few years she has focussed on developing her creative practice. She likes to explore emerging technology and environmental themes in her fiction. In 2018 Deborah received a place in the ACT Writers Centre HARDCOPY program to develop a YA speculative fiction manuscript about remnant nanotechnology in a future Sydney. Since 2019, her flash fiction and short stories have been accepted for Australian-based anthologies from Kirrily King Publishing and Deadset Press. Twitter: @dl_fleming

—

Donna Maree Hanson is a traditionally and independently published author of fantasy, science fiction and horror. She also writes paranormal romance under the pseudonym of Dani Kristoff. In April 2015, she was awarded the A. Bertram Chandler Award for Outstanding Achievement in Australian Science Fiction for her work in running science fiction conventions, publishing and broader SF community contribution. Donna writes dark fantasy (the Dragon Wine series), epic fantasy (the Silverlands series), steampunk (the Cry Havoc series) and young adult science fiction (Space Pirate Adventures) as well as short stories across the speculative fiction genre. Her short story collection, *Beneath the Floating City*, was shortlisted for an Aurealis Award in 2017.

Donna is currently in the final year of her PhD candidature, researching feminism in popular romance at the University of Canberra. Donna lives in Canberra with her partner and fellow writer Matthew Farrer.

—

Alexander Hardison has published short fiction in *Aurealis*, *Capricious* and *The Devilfish Review*. He is a voracious reader of science fiction both serious and fantastical, and spends more time than is healthy online. He lives in Sydney with his partner, cat and comic book collection. Find him on Twitter @euchrid, or spending too much on Steam games he'll never play. If he were a monster, he'd be a dragon because all that sleeping looks very relaxing.

—

Freya Marske lives in Australia, where she is yet to be killed by any form of wildlife. She writes stories full of magic, blood, and as much kissing as she can get away with, and she co-hosts the Hugo-Award-nominated podcast Be the Serpent. Her hobbies include figure skating and discovering new art galleries, and she is on a quest to try all the gin in the world. Her debut novel, the queer historical fantasy *A Marvellous Light*, is forthcoming from Tor.com Publishing in 2021.

Find her on Twitter at @freyamarske, or at freyamarske.com.

—

C.H. Pearce is a sci fi/fantasy writer of weird dystopian stories, mostly with a domestic or workplace focus, banter, and rats. She lives in Canberra with her partner and their toddler and newborn, and works in records management. Her fiction has appeared in *Aurealis*, *Award Winning Australian Writing 2016*, and *A Hand of Knaves*. She is working on more short stories and her first novel. Find her online on chpearce.net, Facebook, Twitter @CHPearceWrites, and Instagram @c.h.pearce.

—

Alannah K. Pearson is a speculative fiction author, combining her interests and expertise in archaeology and ancient history, global folktales, mythologies and environment. Alannah's writing interests include Amerindian folktales, Norse mythology, Prehistory, Archaeology, Ancient History and Gothic folklore. Alannah also has an academic background in Archaeology, Prehistory and human evolution. When not writing, Alannah is completing a PhD in human and primate evolution or enjoying the Australian wilderness with two dogs (canine assistants). She is a keen nature and wildlife photographer, bookshop and museum devotee. You can follow her at alannahkpearson.com and Twitter @AlannahKPearson.

—

Louise Pieper has been told she's too smart for her own good, wears too much black, has too many books and reads too much, but she doesn't believe any of these things are possible. She does believe that stories can change the world. Hers have been published in *Heroines 1* and *2* (Neo Perennial Press, 2018 and 2019) and *A Hand of Knaves* (CSFG Publishing, 2018). Find out more at louisepieper.com.

—

Nathan Phillips is a Canberra-based writer of things that just somehow seem to end up dark. He writes predominantly in fantasy, but dabbles in general and science fiction. He is also a structural editor working with Odyssey Books and is studying a Master of Letters. He lives with a very patient and understanding wife, two very energetic children, and two very indifferent cats. This is his first time being published in the realm of speculative fiction.

—

Rob Porteous is a Canberra writer, editor and teacher of spec-fic. He is currently working on two novels, one fantasy and the other sci-fi.

—

Tansy Rayner Roberts is a Classics graduate gone rogue. She is the author of *Musketeer Space*, the Creature Court trilogy, *Unreal Alchemy* and *Castle Charming*, among many other titles. She has won Hugos for fan writing and podcasting. Find her website at tansyrr.com and her newsletter at: tinyurl.com/tansyrr

—

Ever since she can remember, **Leife Shallcross** has been fascinated by stories about canny fairy godmothers, heroic goose girls and handsome princes disguised as bears. Her debut novel, *The Beast's Heart*, was published by Hodder & Stoughton in May 2018 and her award-winning short fiction has been published in *Aurealis*, *Daily Science Fiction* and several anthologies. She also co-edited the 2018 anthology *A Hand of Knaves* from CSFG Publishing with Chris Large. She is always working on more new novels, just probably not the ones she should be working on.

Ingram Content Group UK Ltd.
Milton Keynes UK
UKHW011510260623
424064UK00004B/107

9 780648 414636